Samuel French Acting Edition

Angel Street

by Patrick Hamilton

Copyright © 1939 by Patrick Hamilton under the title *Gaslight*
Copyright © 1942 (Acting Edition) by Patrick Hamilton
Copyright © 2016 (In Renewal) by Patrick Hamilton
All Rights Reserved

ANGEL STREET is fully protected under the copyright laws of the United States of America, the British Commonwealth, including Canada, and all member countries of the Berne Convention for the Protection of Literary and Artistic Works, the Universal Copyright Convention, and/ or the World Trade Organization conforming to the Agreement on Trade Related Aspects of Intellectual Property Rights. All rights, including professional and amateur stage productions, recitation, lecturing, public reading, motion picture, radio broadcasting, television, online/digital production, and the rights of translation into foreign languages are strictly reserved.

ISBN 978-0-573-60535-2

www.concordtheatricals.com
www.concordtheatricals.co.uk

FOR PRODUCTION INQUIRIES

UNITED STATES AND CANADA
info@concordtheatricals.com
1-866-979-0447

UNITED KINGDOM AND EUROPE
licensing@concordtheatricals.co.uk
020-7054-7200

Each title is subject to availability from Concord Theatricals Corp., depending upon country of performance. Please be aware that *ANGEL STREET* may not be licensed by Concord Theatricals Corp. in your territory. Professional and amateur producers should contact the nearest Concord Theatricals Corp. office or licensing partner to verify availability.

CAUTION: Professional and amateur producers are hereby warned that *ANGEL STREET* is subject to a licensing fee. The purchase, renting, lending or use of this book does not constitute a license to perform this title(s), which license must be obtained from Concord Theatricals Corp. prior to any performance. Performance of this title(s) without a license is a violation of federal law and may subject the producer and/or presenter of such performances to civil penalties. Both amateurs and professionals considering a production are strongly advised to apply to the appropriate agent before starting rehearsals, advertising, or booking a theatre. A licensing fee must be paid whether the title(s) is presented for charity or gain and whether or not admission is charged. Professional/Stock licensing fees are quoted upon application to Concord Theatricals Corp.

This work is published by Samuel French, an imprint of Concord Theatricals Corp.

No one shall make any changes in this title(s) for the purpose of production. No part of this book may be reproduced, stored in a retrieval system, scanned, uploaded, or transmitted in any form, by any means, now known or yet to be invented, including mechanical, electronic, digital, photocopying, recording, videotaping, or otherwise, without the prior written permission of the publisher. No one shall share this title(s), or any part of this title(s), through any social media or file hosting websites.

For all inquiries regarding motion picture, television, online/digital and other media rights, please contact Concord Theatricals Corp.

MUSIC AND THIRD-PARTY MATERIALS USE NOTE

Licensees are solely responsible for obtaining formal written permission from copyright owners to use copyrighted music and/or other copyrighted third-party materials (e.g., artworks, logos) in the performance of this play and are strongly cautioned to do so. If no such permission is obtained by the licensee, then the licensee must use only original music and materials that the licensee owns and controls. Licensees are solely responsible and liable for clearances of all third-party copyrighted materials, including without limitation music, and shall indemnify the copyright owners of the play(s) and their licensing agent, Concord Theatricals Corp., against any costs, expenses, losses and liabilities arising from the use of such copyrighted third-party materials by licensees. For music, please contact the appropriate music licensing authority in your territory for the rights to any incidental music.

IMPORTANT BILLING AND CREDIT REQUIREMENTS

If you have obtained performance rights to this title, please refer to your licensing agreement for important billing and credit requirements.

Copy of program of the first performance of *"Angel Street"*
as produced at the John Golden Theatre, New York.

SHEPARD TRAUBE

(IN ASSOCIATION WITH ALEXANDER H. COHEN)

PRESENTS

ANGEL STREET

A VICTORIAN THRILLER BY

PATRICK HAMILTON

STAGED BY MR. TRAUBE

CAST

(In order of appearance)

MRS. MANNINGHAM.....................*Judith Evelyn*

MR. MANNINGHAM.....................*Vincent Price*

NANCY.............................*Elizabeth Eustis*

ELIZABETH..........................*Florence Edney*

ROUGH.............................*Leo G. Carroll*

The entire action of the play occurs in a house on Angel Street,
located in the Pimlico district of London. The time is 1880.

ACT ONE
Late afternoon.

ACT TWO
Immediately afterwards.

ACT THREE
Later the same night.

"Angel Street" was first presented under the title, *"Gas Light,"* by Gardner Davies, on December 5, 1938, at the Richmond Theatre, Richmond, London, England, with the following cast:

MRS. MANNINGHAM...........*Gwen Ffrangcon-Davies*

MR. MANNINGHAM...................*Dennis Arundell*

ROUGH...............................*Milton Rosmer*

ELIZABETH...........................*Beatrice Rowe*

NANCY ....*Elizabeth Inglis*

STORY OF THE PLAY

IT tells the demoniac story of the Manninghams of Angel Street. Under the guise of kindliness, handsome Mr. Manningham is torturing his wife into insanity. He accuses her of petty aberrations that he has arranged himself; and since her mother died of insanity, she is more than half convinced that she, too, is going out of her mind. While her diabolical husband is out of the house, a benign police inspector visits her and ultimately proves to her that her husband is a maniacal criminal suspected of a murder committed fifteen years ago in the same house, and that he is preparing to dispose of her. Then starts the game of trying to uncover the necessary evidence against Mr. Manningham. It is a thrilling and exciting melodramatic game.

DESCRIPTION OF CHARACTERS

MR. MANNINGHAM. He is tall, good-looking, about forty-five. He is heavily moustached and bearded and perhaps a little too well dressed. His manner is suave and authoritative, with a touch of mystery and bitterness.

MRS. MANNINGHAM. She is about thirty-four. She has been good-looking, almost a beauty—but now she has a haggard, wan, frightened air, with rings under her eyes, which tell of sleepless nights and worse.

ELIZABETH. She is a stout, amiable, subservient woman of fifty.

NANCY. She is a self-conscious, pretty, cheeky girl of nineteen.

ROUGH. He is middle-aged—greying, short, wiry, active, brusque, friendly, overbearing. He has a low, warm chuckle and completely dominates the scene from the beginning.

ACT ONE

ACT ONE

The scene is a living-room on the first floor of a four-storied house in a gloomy and unfashionable quarter of London, in the latter part of the last century. The room is furnished in all the heavily draped and dingy profusion of the period, and yet, amidst this abundance of paraphernalia, an air is breathed of poverty, wretchedness and age.

Fireplace down Right. Door at Right above fireplace leading to little room. Settee Right, Left of fireplace with stool in front of it. Table Center with chairs Right and Left of it. Window at Left. Desk in front of window with chairs back and above it. Secretary against wall up Right. Lamp on table Center. Sliding double doors at back Left Center leading to hall, to Left the front door, to Right the servants quarters. A circular stair leading to the upper floors is at back up Right Center. Chairs down Right and Left.

The Curtain rises upon the rather terrifying darkness of the late afternoon—the zero hour, as it were, before the feeble dawn of gas light and tea. In front of the fire, on the sofa MANNINGHAM *is stretched out and sleeping heavily. He is tall, good-looking, about forty-five. He is heavily moustached and bearded and perhaps a little too well dressed. His manner is suave and authoritative, with a touch of mystery and bitterness.* MRS. MANNING-HAM *is sitting sewing on the chair Left of the Center table. She is about thirty-four. She has been good-look-*

3

ing, almost a beauty—but now she has a haggard, wan, frightened air, with rings under her eyes, which tell of sleepless nights and worse. Big Ben strikes five. The Curtain rises.

Pause. From the street below, in the distance, can be heard the intermittent jingling of a muffin-man ringing his bell.

MRS. MANNINGHAM *listens to this sound for a few moments, furtively and indecisively, almost as though she is frightened even of this. Then she looks toward the sound down in the street. Then to the bell-cord by the Left Center door, which she pulls. Then back to her sewing, which she gathers up and puts into a box, at the same time taking a purse therefrom. There is a knock at the door, and* ELIZABETH, *the cook and housekeeper, enters. She is a stout, amiable, subservient woman of about fifty. Signalling that her husband is asleep,* MRS. MANNINGHAM *goes over and whispers to her at the door, giving her some money from the purse.* ELIZABETH *goes out closing the doors.*

MR. MANNINGHAM. [*Whose eyes have opened, but whose position has not changed a fraction of an inch.*] What are you doing, Bella?

MRS. MANNINGHAM. Nothing, dear— [MRS. MANNINGHAM *crosses quietly and quickly to the secretary with her sewing and starts back to the doors.*] Don't wake yourself. [*There is a pause. She starts to window.*]

MR. MANNINGHAM. [*Whose eyes are closed again.*] What *are* you doing, Bella? Come here—

MRS. MANNINGHAM. [*After hesitating, going to him.*] Only for tea, my dear. Muffins—for tea— [*She takes his hand.*]

MR. MANNINGHAM. Muffins—eh—?

MRS. MANNINGHAM. Yes, dear— He only comes so seldom—I thought I might surprise you.

MR. MANNINGHAM. Why are you so apprehensive, Bella? I was not about to reproach you.

MRS. MANNINGHAM. [*Nervously releasing her hand.*] No, dear. I know you weren't.

MR. MANNINGHAM. That fire's in ashes. Ring the bell, will you, Bella dear, please?

MRS. MANNINGHAM. Yes— [*Is going over to bell, but stops.*] Is it merely to put coal on, my dear? I can do that.

MR. MANNINGHAM. Now then, Bella. We've had this out before. Be so good as to ring the bell.

MRS. MANNINGHAM. But, dear—Lizzie's out in the street. Let me do it. I can do it so easily. [*She comes over to do it.*]

MR. MANNINGHAM. [*Stopping her with outstretched hand.*] No, no, no, no, no— Where's the girl? Let the girl come up if Lizzie's out.

MRS. MANNINGHAM. But, my dear—

MR. MANNINGHAM. Go and ring the bell, please, Bella— there's a good child. [MRS. MANNINGHAM *gives in, and goes back to ring the bell.*] Now, come here. [*She does so.*] What do you suppose the servants are for, Bella? [MRS. MANNINGHAM *does not answer. There is a pause; then gently,*] Go on. Answer me. [*He rises.*] What do you suppose servants are for?

MRS. MANNINGHAM. [*Shamefacedly, and scarcely audible, merely dutifully feeding him.*] To serve us, I suppose, Jack—

MR. MANNINGHAM. Precisely. Then why—?

MRS. MANNINGHAM. But I think we should consider them a little, that's all.

MR. MANNINGHAM. Consider them? There's your extraordinary confusion of mind again. You speak as though they work for no consideration. I happen to consider Elizabeth to the tune of sixteen pounds per annum. [*Crosses to* MRS. MANNINGHAM.] And the girl ten. Twenty-six pounds a year all told. And if that is not consideration of the most acute and lively kind, I should like to know what is.

MRS. MANNINGHAM. Yes, Jack. I expect you are right.

MR. MANNINGHAM. I have no doubt of it, my dear. It's sheer weak-mindedness to think otherwise. [*Pause as he crosses and looks in the mirror and she crosses to window and looks out into the street.*] What's the weather doing? Is it still as yellow?

MRS. MANNINGHAM. Yes, it seems to be denser than ever. Shall you be going out in this, Jack dear?

MR. MANNINGHAM. Oh—I expect so. Unless it gets very much worse after tea. [*There is a KNOCK at the door.* MRS. MANNINGHAM *hesitates. There is another knock.*] Come in. [*He crosses and sits on sofa.*]

[*Enter* NANCY, *the maid. She is a self-conscious, pretty, cheeky girl of nineteen. He turns and looks at* MRS. MANNINGHAM.]

NANCY. [*Stands looking at* BOTH, *as* MRS. MANNING-HAM *hesitates to tell her why she rang the bell.*] Oh, I beg your pardon. I thought the bell rang—

MR. MANNINGHAM. Yes, we rang the bell, Nancy— [*Pause.*] Go on, my dear, tell her why we rang the bell.

MRS. MANNINGHAM. Oh— Yes— We want some coal on the fire, Nancy, please.

[NANCY *looks at her impudently, and then, with a little smile and toss of the head, goes over to put coal on the fire.*]

MR. MANNINGHAM. [*After pause.*] And you might as well light the gas, Nancy. This darkness in the afternoon is getting beyond endurance.

NANCY. Yes, sir. [*With another barely discernible little smile, she gets the matches, and goes to light the two incandescent mantles on each side of the fireplace.*]

MR. MANNINGHAM. [*Watches her as she lights the second mantle.*] You're looking very impudent and pretty this afternoon, Nancy. Do you know that?

NANCY. I don't know at all, sir, I'm sure.

MR. MANNINGHAM. What is it? Another broken heart added to your list?

NANCY I wasn't aware of breaking any hearts, sir.

MR. MANNINGHAM. I'm sure that's not true. And that complexion of yours. That's not true, either. I wonder what mysterious lotions you've been employing to enhance your natural beauties.

NANCY. I'm quite natural, sir, I promise you [*Crosses to light lamp on Center table.*]

MR. MANNINGHAM. But you do it adroitly, I grant you that. What are your secrets? Won't you tell us the name of your chemist? Perhaps you could pass it on to Mrs. Manningham—[*A quick look by* NANCY *at* MRS. MANNINGHAM.] and help banish her pallor. She would be most grateful, I have no doubt.

NANCY. I'd be most happy to, I'm sure, sir.

MR. MANNINGHAM. Or are women too jealous of their discoveries to pass them on to a rival?

NANCY. I don't know, sir— Will that be all you're wanting, sir?

MR. MANNINGHAM. Yes. That's all I want, Nancy— [*She stops.*] Except my tea.

NANCY. It'll be coming directly, sir. [*Goes out Left Center and leaves door open.*]

MRS. MANNINGHAM. [*After a pause, reproachfully rather than angrily, moving to below table.*] Oh, Jack, how can you treat me like that?

MR. MANNINGHAM. But, my dear, you're the mistress of the house. It was your business to tell her to put the coal on.

MRS. MANNINGHAM. It *isn't* that! It's humiliating me like that. As though I'd do anything to my face, and ask for *her* assistance if I did.

MR. MANNINGHAM. But you seem to look on servants as our natural equals. So I treated her as one. [*Pause as he sits down on settee and picks up newspaper.*] Besides, I was only trifling with her.

MRS. MANNINGHAM. It's strange that you can't see how

you hurt me. That girl laughs at me enough already.

MR. MANNINGHAM. Laughs at you? What an idea. What makes you think she laughs at you?

MRS. MANNINGHAM. Oh—I know that she does in secret. In fact, she does so openly—more openly every day.

MR. MANNINGHAM. But, my dear—if she does that, doesn't the fault lie with you?

MRS. MANNINGHAM. [*Pause.*] You mean that I'm a laughable person?

MR. MANNINGHAM. I don't mean anything. It's you who read meanings into everything, Bella dear. I wish you weren't such a perfect little silly. Come here and stop it. I've just thought of something rather nice.

MRS. MANNINGHAM. Something nice? What have you thought of, Jack?

MR. MANNINGHAM. I shan't tell you unless you come here.

MRS. MANNINGHAM. [*Going over and sitting on chair Right of table.*] What is it, Jack? What have you thought of?

MR. MANNINGHAM. I read here that Mr. MacNaughton —the celebrated actor—is in London for another season.

MRS. MANNINGHAM. Yes. I read that. What of it, Jack?

MR. MANNINGHAM. What of it? What do you suppose?

MRS. MANNINGHAM. Oh, Jack dear. Do you mean it? Would you take me to see MacNaughton? You wouldn't take me to see MacNaughton, would you?

MR. MANNINGHAM. I not only would take you to see MacNaughton, my dear. I am going to take you to see MacNaughton. That is, if you want to go.

MRS. MANNINGHAM. [*Rises.*] Oh, Jack! What heaven—what heaven!

MR. MANNINGHAM. When would you like to go? You have only three weeks, according to his advertisement.

MRS. MANNINGHAM. [*To back of sofa and over* MR. MANNINGHAM'S *shoulder.*] Oh—what perfect heaven! Let me see. Do let me see!

MR. MANNINGHAM. There. You see? You can see him in comedy or tragedy—according to your choice. Which would you prefer, Bella—the comedy or the tragedy?

MRS. MANNINGHAM. Oh—it's so hard to say! Either would be equally wonderful. [*Crosses around back of settee to Right end and below.*] Which would you choose, if you were me?

MR. MANNINGHAM. Well—it depends—doesn't it—upon whether you want to laugh, or whether you want to cry.

MRS. MANNINGHAM. Oh—I want to laugh. But then, I should like to cry, too. In fact, I should like to do both. Oh, Jack, what made you decide to take me? [*Sits on stool and leans against* MR. MANNINGHAM.]

MR. MANNINGHAM. Well, my dear, you've been very good lately, and I thought it would be well to take you out of yourself.

MRS. MANNINGHAM. Oh, Jack dear. You have been so

much kinder lately. Is it possible you're beginning to see my point of view?

MR. MANNINGHAM. I don't know that I ever differed from it, did I, Bella?

MRS. MANNINGHAM. Oh, Jack dear. It's true. It's true. [*Looks at him.*] All I need is to be taken out of myself —some little change—to have some attention from you. Oh, Jack, I'd be better,—I could really try to be better— you know in what way—if only I could get *out* of myself a little more.

MR. MANNINGHAM. How do you mean, my dear, exactly, *better?*

MRS. MANNINGHAM. [*Looks away.*] You know— You know in what way, dear. About all that's happened lately. We said we wouldn't speak about it.

MR. MANNINGHAM. [*Drawing away and looking away.*] Oh, no—don't let's speak about that.

MRS. MANNINGHAM. No, dear, I don't want to—but what I say is so important. I *have* been better—even in the last week. Haven't you noticed it? And why is it? Because you have stayed in, and been kind to me. The other night when you stayed in and played cards with me, it was like old days, and I went to bed feeling a normal, happy, healthy, human being. And then, the day after, when you read your book to me, Jack, and we sat by the fire, I felt all my love for you coming back, then, Jack. And I slept that night like a child. All those ghastly dreads and terrible, terrible fears seemed to have vanished. And all just because you had given me your time, and taken me from brooding on myself in this house all day and night.

MR. MANNINGHAM. [*As he raises up her head off his shoulder.*] I wonder if it is that—or whether it's merely that your medicine is beginning to benefit you?

MRS. MANNINGHAM. No, Jack dear, it's not my medicine. I've taken my medicine religiously—haven't I taken it religiously? Much as I detest it! It's more than medicine that I want. It's the medicine of a sweet, sane mind, of interest in something. Don't you see what I mean?

MR. MANNINGHAM. Well—we *are* talking about gloomy subjects, aren't we?

MRS. MANNINGHAM. [*Sitting on settee.*] Yes. I don't want to be gloomy, dear—that's the last thing I want to be. I only want you to understand. Say you understand.

MR. MANNINGHAM. [*Turns to her.*] Well, dear. Don't I seem to? Haven't I just said I'm taking you to the theatre?

MRS. MANNINGHAM. [*Close to him again.*] Yes, dear— Yes, you have. Oh, and you've made me so happy—so happy, dear.

MR. MANNINGHAM. Well, then, which is it to be—the comedy or the tragedy. You must make up your mind.

MRS. MANNINGHAM. [*With exulting solemnity.*] Oh, Jack, which shall it be? [*Rising and crossing to down Center and showing her pleasure with delighted gestures.*] What *shall* it be? It matters so little! It matters so wonderfully little! I'm going to the play! [*To Left Center then to back of Center table and to back of settee and throws her arms around him and kisses him.*] Do

you understand that, my husband! I'm going to the play!
[*There is a KNOCK on the Left Center door.* MRS.
MANNINGHAM *crosses to the fireplace.*] Come in. [*Enter* NANCY, *carrying tray. Pause, as she starts to desk
Left.*] No, Nancy, I think we'll have it on the table today.

NANCY. [*Still with impudence.*] Oh—just as you wish,
Madam.

[*Pause, as she puts tray on table Center, arranges cups
and puts books, etc., on one side.*]

MRS. MANNINGHAM. [*At mantelpiece.*] Tell me, Nancy
—if you were being taken to the play, and had to choose
between comedy and tragedy, which would *you* choose?

NANCY. No, Madam? Oh—I'd go for the comedy all
the time.

MRS. MANNINGHAM. Would you? Why would you
choose the comedy, Nancy?

NANCY. I like to laugh, Madam, I suppose.

MRS. MANNINGHAM. Do you? Well—I daresay you're
right. I must bear it in mind. Mr. Manningham's taking
me next week, you see.

NANCY. Oh, yes? I hope you enjoy it. I'll bring the muffins directly. [*Goes out, leaves the doors open, and turns
to the Right.*]

[*As* NANCY *goes out,* MRS. MANNINGHAM *puts out her
tongue at her.* MANNINGHAM *sees this.*]

MR. MANNINGHAM. My dear—what are you doing?

MRS. MANNINGHAM. [*As she crosses to the foot of the*

stairs.] The little beast! Let her put that in her pipe and smoke it.

MR. MANNINGHAM. But what has she done?

MRS. MANNINGHAM. Ah—you don't know her. She tries to torment and score off me all day long. You don't see these things. A man wouldn't. [MR. MANNINGHAM *rises.*] She thinks me a poor thing. And now she can suffer the news that you're taking me to the theatre.

MR. MANNINGHAM. I think you imagine things, my dear.

MRS. MANNINGHAM. Oh, no, I don't. We've been too familiar with her. [*Arranging chairs, in an emotionally happy state.*] Come along, my dear. You sit one side, and I the other—like two children in the nursery.

MR. MANNINGHAM. [*Stands with back to fire.*] You seem wonderfully pleased with yourself, Bella. I must take you to the theatre more often, if this is the result.

MRS. MANNINGHAM. [*Sitting Left of table.*] Oh, Jack— I wish you could.

MR. MANNINGHAM. I don't really know why we shouldn't. I used to like nothing so much when I was a boy. In fact, you may hardly believe it, but I even had an ambition to be an actor myself at one time.

MRS. MANNINGHAM. [*Lifting tea pot.*] I can well believe it, dear. Come along to your tea now.

MR. MANNINGHAM. [*As he moves up back of the settee.*] You know, Bella, that must be a very superb sensation. To take a part and lose yourself entirely in the character of someone else. I flatter myself I could have made an actor.

MRS. MANNINGHAM. [*Pouring tea.*] Why, of course, my dear. You were cut out for it. Anyone can see that.

MR. MANNINGHAM. [*Crosses slowly Left behind settee.*] No—do you think so—seriously? I always felt a faint tinge of regret. Of course, one would have required training, but I believe I should have made out— and might have reached the top of the tree for all I know.
"To be or not to be. That is the question.
Whether 'tis nobler in the mind to suffer
The slings and arrows of outrageous fortune,
Or to take arms—against a sea of troubles,
And, by opposing, end them."

[NANCY *enters, sets the muffin dish down on table during the recitation and goes out.*]

MRS. MANNINGHAM. [*After* NANCY *exits.*] You see how fine your voice is? Oh—you've made a great mistake.

MR. MANNINGHAM. [*Crosses to Right of table. Lightly.*] I wonder.

MRS. MANNINGHAM. Then if you had been a famous actor, I should have had a free seat to come and watch you every night of my life. And then called for you at the stage door afterwards. Wouldn't that have been paradise?

MR. MANNINGHAM. [*As he sits Right of table.*] A paradise of which you would soon tire, my dear. I have no doubt that after a few nights you would be staying at home again, just as you do now.

MRS. MANNINGHAM. Oh, no, I wouldn't. I should have

to keep my eye on you for all the hussies that would be after you.

MR. MANNINGHAM. There would be hussies after me, would there? That is an added inducement, then.

MRS. MANNINGHAM. Yes—I know it, you wretch. But you wouldn't escape me. [*Lifting cover of muffin dish.*] They look delicious. Aren't you glad I thought of them? [*Passes the salt.*] Here's some salt. You want heaps of it. Oh, Jack dear, you must forgive me chattering on like this, but I'm feeling so happy.

MR. MANNINGHAM. I can see that, my dear.

MRS. MANNINGHAM. I'm being taken to the play, you see. Here you are. I used to adore these as a child, didn't you? [*Offers muffin to* MR. MANNINGHAM.] I wonder how long it is since we had them? [MR. MANNINGHAM *looks up Center at wall.*] We haven't had them since we've been married anyway. Or have we? Have we?

MR. MANNINGHAM. I don't know, I'm sure. [*Suddenly rising, looking at the wall upstage and speaking in a calm, yet menacing way.*] I don't know—Bella—

MRS. MANNINGHAM. [*After pause, dropping her voice almost to a whisper.*] What is it? What's the matter? What is it now?

MR. MANNINGHAM. [*Walking over to fireplace in front of settee, and speaking with his back to her.*] I have no desire to upset you, Bella, but I have just observed something very much amiss. Will you please rectify it at once, while I am not looking, and we will assume that it has not happened.

MRS. MANNINGHAM. Amiss? What's amiss? For God's

sake don't turn your back on me. What has happened?

MR. MANNINGHAM. You know perfectly well what has happened, Bella, and if you will rectify it at once I will say no more about it.

MRS. MANNINGHAM. I don't know. I don't know. You have left your tea. Tell me what it is. Tell me.

MR. MANNINGHAM. Are you trying to make a fool of me, Bella? What I refer to is on the wall behind you. If you will put it back, I will say no more about it.

MRS. MANNINGHAM. The wall behind me? What? [*Turns.*] Oh—yes— The picture has been taken down — Yes— The picture— Who has taken it down? Why has it been taken down?

MR. MANNINGHAM. Yes. Why has it been taken down? Why, indeed. You alone can answer that, Bella. Why was it taken down before? Will you please take it from wherever you have hidden it, and put it back on the wall again?

MRS. MANNINGHAM. But I haven't hidden it, Jack. [*Rises.*] I didn't do it. Oh, for God's sake look at me. I didn't do it. I don't know where it is. Someone else must have done it.

MR. MANNINGHAM. Someone else? [*Turning to her.*] Are you suggesting perhaps that I should play such a fantastic and wicked trick?

MRS. MANNINGHAM. No, dear, no! But someone else. [*Going to him.*] Before God, I didn't do it! Someone else, dear, someone else.

MR. MANNINGHAM. [*Shaking her off.*] Will you please

leave go of me. [*Walking over to bell.*] We will see about "someone else."

MRS. MANNINGHAM. [*Crossing to front of settee.*] Oh, Jack—don't ring the bell. Don't ring it. Don't call the servants to witness my shame. It's not my shame for I haven't done it—but *don't* call the servants! Tell them not to come. [*He has rung the bell. She goes to him.*] Let's talk of this between ourselves! Don't call that girl in. Please!

MR. MANNINGHAM. [*Shaking her off violently.*] Will you please leave go of me and sit down there! [*She sits in chair above the desk. He goes to fireplace.*] Someone else, eh? Well—we shall see. [MRS. MANNINGHAM *in chair, sobs.*] You had better pull yourself together, hadn't you?—[*There is a KNOCK at the door.*] Come in. [*Enter* ELIZABETH *Left Center and leaves the doors open.*] Ah, Elizabeth. Come in please, Elizabeth— Shut the door—[*Pause as she does so.*] well, come in, come into the room.—[*Pause as* ELIZABETH *crosses to the back of the chair Left of the table.*] Now, Elizabeth, do you notice anything amiss in this room?—Look carefully around the walls, and see if you notice anything amiss— [*Pause as* ELIZABETH *looks around the room and when she sees the space of the missing picture she stands still.*] Well, Elizabeth, what do you notice?

ELIZABETH. Nothing, sir— Except the picture's been taken down.

MR. MANNINGHAM. Exactly. The picture has been taken down. You noticed it at once. Now was that picture in its place when you dusted the room this morning?

ELIZABETH. Yes, sir. It was, sir. I don't understand, sir.

MR. MANNINGHAM. Neither do I, Elizabeth, neither do I. And now, before you go, just one question. Was it you who removed that picture, Elizabeth?

ELIZABETH. No, sir. Of course I ain't, sir.

MR. MANNINGHAM. You did not. And have you ever, at any time, removed that picture from its proper place?

ELIZABETH. No, sir. Never, sir. Why should I, sir?

MR. MANNINGHAM. Indeed, why should you?—And now please, Elizabeth, will you kiss that Bible, will you as a token of your truthfulness—fetch that Bible from my desk? [*Pause.* ELIZABETH *hesitates. Then she does so.*] Very well, you may go. [*She starts to the desk with Bible and* MANNINGHAM *motions to her to put it on Center table.*] And please send Nancy in here at once.

ELIZABETH. Yes, sir. [*Opens doors, goes out, closes doors, looking at* BOTH.]

MRS. MANNINGHAM. [*Going to him.*] Jack—spare me that girl. Don't call her in. I'll say anything. I'll say that I did it. I did it, Jack, I did it. Don't have that girl in. Don't!

MR. MANNINGHAM. Will you have the goodness to contain yourself? [*There is a KNOCK at the Left Center door.* MRS. MANNINGHAM *sits in chair below fireplace.*] Come in.

NANCY. [*Opens doors, enters and leaves doors open. Crossing to settee.*] Yes, sir. Did you want me?

MR. MANNINGHAM. Yes, I do want you, Nancy.—If you will look at the wall behind you, you will see that the picture has gone

NANCY. [*Going up-tage.*] Why. My word. So it has. [*Turns.*] What a rum go! [*Turns to* MANNINGHAM.]

MR. MANNINGHAM. I did not ask for any comment on your part, Nancy. Kindly be less insolent and answer what I ask you. Did *you* take that picture down, or did you not?

NANCY. Me? Of course I didn't. [*Comes to him slyly.*] What should I want to move it for, sir?

MR. MANNINGHAM. Very good. Now will you kiss that Bible lying there, please, as a solemn oath that you did not—and you may go.

NANCY. Willingly, sir. [*She does so, and places Bible on Center table again with a little smile.*] If I'd done it I'd've—

MR. MANNINGHAM. That is all, Nancy. You may go. [NANCY *goes out and closes doors. Going to Bible as if to replace it on the desk.*] There! [*As he crosses down Left and faces* MRS. MANNINGHAM.] I think we may now be said to have demonstrated conclusively—

MRS. MANNINGHAM. [*Rises; crossing Left to him.*] Give me that Bible! Give it to me! Let me kiss it, too! [*Snatches it from him.*] There! [*Kisses it.*] There! Do you see? [*Kisses it.*] There! Do you see that I kiss it?

MR. MANNINGHAM. [*As he puts out his hand for the Bible.*] For God's sake be careful what you do. Do you desire to commit sacrilege above all else?

MRS. MANNINGHAM. It is no sacrilege, Jack. Someone else has committed sacrilege. Now see—I swear before God Almighty that I never touched that picture. [*Kisses it.*] There! [*She comes close to him.*]

MR. MANNINGHAM. [*He grabs Bible.*] Then, by God, you are mad, and you don't know what you do. You unhappy wretch—you're stark gibbering mad—like your wretched mother before you.

MRS. MANNINGHAM. Jack—you promised you would never say that again.

MR. MANNINGHAM. [*Crosses Right. Pause.*] The time has come to face facts, Bella. [*Half turns to her.*] If this progresses you will not be much longer under *my* protection.

MRS. MANNINGHAM. [*Crossing to him.*] Jack—I'm going to make a last appeal to you. I'm going to make a last appeal. I'm desperate, Jack. Can't you see that I'm desperate? If you can't, you must have a heart of stone.

MR. MANNINGHAM. [*Turns to her.*] Go on. What do you wish to say?

MRS. MANNINGHAM. Jack, [*Crosses to front of settee.*] I may be going mad, like my poor mother—but if I am mad, you have got to treat me gently. Jack—before God —I never lie to you knowingly. If I have taken down that picture from its place I have not known it. *I have not known it.* If I took it down on those other occasions I did not know it, either. [*Turns and crosses to Center.*] Jack, if I steal your things—your rings—your keys— your pencils and your handkerchiefs, and you find them later at the bottom of my box, as indeed you do, then I do not know that I have done it— Jack, if I commit these fantastic, meaningless mischiefs—so meaningless —[*A step toward him.*] why should I take a picture down from its place? [*Pause.*] If I do all these things, then I am certainly going off my head, and must be treated kindly and gently so that I may get well. [*Crosses to him.*] You must *bear* with me, Jack, *bear* with me—not storm and rage. God knows I'm trying, Jack, I'm trying! Oh, for God's sake believe me that I'm trying and be kind to me!

MR. MANNINGHAM. Bella, my dear—have you any idea where that picture is now?

MRS. MANNINGHAM. Yes, yes, I suppose it's behind the cupboard.

MR. MANNINGHAM. Will you please go and see?

MRS. MANNINGHAM. [*Vaguely.*] Yes—yes— [*Crosses below him, goes Right to upper end of secretary and produces it.*] Yes, it's here.

MR. MANNINGHAM. [*Reproachfully. As he crosses to the desk, places the Bible on it and crosses up Left.*] Then you did know where it was, Bella. [*Turns to her.*] You did know where it was.

MRS. MANNINGHAM. [*As she starts toward him.*] No! No! I only *supposed* it was! I only supposed it was because it was found there before! It was found there twice before. Don't you see? I *didn't* know—I didn't!

MR. MANNINGHAM. There is no sense in walking about the room with a picture in your hands, Bella. Go and put it back in its proper place.

MRS. MANNINGHAM. [*Pause as she hangs the picture on wall—she comes to the back of the chair Right of table.*] Oh, look at our tea. We were having our tea with muffins—

MR. MANNINGHAM. Now, Bella, I said a moment ago

that we have got to face facts. And that is what we have got to do. I am not going to say anything at the moment, for my feelings are running too high. In fact, I am going out immediately, and I suggest that you go to your room and lie down for a little in the dark.

MRS. MANNINGHAM. No, no—not my room. For God's sake don't send me to my room! [*Grabbing chair.*]

MR. MANNINGHAM. There is no question of sending you to your room, Bella. [*Crosses to her.*] You know perfectly well that you may do exactly as you please.

MRS. MANNINGHAM. I feel faint, Jack— [*He goes quickly to her and supports her.*] I feel faint—

MR. MANNINGHAM. Very well— [*Leading her to settee and she sinks down with her head to Left end.*] Now, take things quietly and come and lie down, here. Where are your salts? [*Crosses to secretary, gets salts and returns to her back of settee.*] Here they are— [*Pause.*] Now, my dear, I am going to leave you in peace—

MRS. MANNINGHAM. [*Eyes closed, reclining.*] Have you got to go? Must you go? Must you always leave me alone after these dreadful scenes?

MR. MANNINGHAM. Now, no argument, please. I had to go in any case after tea, and I'm merely leaving you a little earlier, that's all. [*Pause. Going into wardrobe and returning with undercoat on.*] Now is there anything I can get for you?

MRS. MANNINGHAM. No, Jack dear, nothing. You go.

MR. MANNINGHAM. Very good— [*Goes toward his hat and overcoat which is on the chair above desk, and stops.*] Oh, by the way, I shall be passing the grocer and

I might as well pay that bill of his and get it done with. Where is it, my dear? I gave it to you, didn't I?

MRS. MANNINGHAM. Yes, dear. It's on the secretary. [*Half rising.*] I'll—

MR. MANNINGHAM. [*Crossing to secretary.*] No, dear —don't move—don't move I can find it. [*At secretary and begins to rummage.*] I shall be glad to get the thing off my chest. Where is it, dear? Is it in one of these drawers?

MRS. MANNINGHAM. No—it's on top. I put it there this afternoon.

MR. MANNINGHAM. All right. We'll find it— We'll find it— Are you sure it's here, dear? There's nothing here except some writing paper.

MRS. MANNINGHAM. [*Half rising and speaking suspiciously.*] Jack, I'm quite sure it *is* there. Will you look carefully?

MR. MANNINGHAM. [*Soothingly.*] All right, dear. Don't worry. I'll find it. Lie down. It's of no importance. I'll find it— No, it's not here— It must be in one of the drawers—

MRS. MANNINGHAM. [*She has rushed to the secretary.*] It is not in one of the drawers! I put it out here on top! You're not going to tell me *this* has gone, are you?

MR. MANNINGHAM. [*Speaking at the same time.*] My dear. Calm yourself. Calm yourself.

}[*Together*]

MRS. MANNINGHAM. [*Searching frantically.*] I laid it out here myself! Where is it? [*Opening and shutting drawers.*] Where is it? Now you're going to say I've hidden this!

MR. MANNINGHAM. [*Walking away to Left end of settee.*] My God!—What new trick is this you're playing upon me?

MRS. MANNINGHAM. [*At Right lower end of settee.*] It was there this afternoon! I put it there! This is a plot! This is a filthy plot! You're all against me! It's a plot! [*She screams hysterically.*]

MR. MANNINGHAM. [*Coming to her and shaking her violently.*] Will you control yourself! Will you control yourself! [*Pause until she calms down.*] Listen to me, Madam, if you utter another sound I'll knock you down and take you to your room and lock you in darkness for a week. I have been too lenient with you, and I mean to alter my tactics.

MRS. MANNINGHAM. [*Sinks to her knees.*] Oh, God help me! God help me!

MR. MANNINGHAM. May God help you, indeed Now listen to me. I am going to leave you until ten o'clock. [*He lifts her up.*] In that time you will recover that paper, and admit to me that you have lyingly and purposely concealed it—if not, you will take the consequences. [*Pause as he places her in the chair down Right and he crosses Left to above desk.*] You are going to see a doctor, [*He stops and turns to* BELLA.] Madam. more than one doctor—[*Puts his hat on and throws his coat over his arm.*] and they shall decide what this means. Now do you understand me?

MRS. MANNINGHAM. Oh, God—be patient with me. If I am mad, be patient with me.

MR. MANNINGHAM. I have been patient with you and controlled myself long enough. It is now for you to control yourself, or take the consequences. Think upon that, Bella. [*Goes to Left Center doors and opens them.*]

MRS. MANNINGHAM. Jack—Jack—don't go—Jack— You're still going to take me to the theatre, aren't you?

MR. MANNINGHAM. What a question to ask me at such a time. No, Madam, emphatically, I am not. You play fair by me, and I'll play fair by you. But if we are going to be enemies, you and I, you will not prosper, believe me. [*Goes out.*]

[*Short pause and then a DOOR slams. Whimperingly,* MRS. MANNINGHAM *rises, aiding herself by the mantel and crosses up to the secretary searching through the drawers, then crosses to Center, looks at the picture at up Center and shudders. Then turning to Center table, she takes up the pitcher of water from the tea tray, crosses to the secretary, opens the upper door of the secretary, gets a glass, then opens a drawer and takes out a paper of medicine. She takes this medicine and follows it with a drink of water. This is obviously, incredibly nasty and almost chokes her. She staggers over to the Center table and replaces the pitcher of water and then turns down the table lamp. Then crossing to the settee, she sinks down on it with her head toward the fireplace and sobs. She mutters, "Peace—Peace—Peace." She breathes heavily as a CLOCK in the house strikes 6.00. Pause. There is a KNOCK at the door. She does not hear it. There is another KNOCK and* ELIZABETH *enters Left Center.*]

ELIZABETH. Madam—Madam— [*She crosses down to back of settee.*]

MRS. MANNINGHAM. Yes!—Yes!—What is it, Elizabeth? Leave me alone.

ELIZABETH. [*Peering through the darkness.*] Madam, there's somebody called.

MRS. MANNINGHAM. Who is it? I don't want to be disturbed.

ELIZABETH. It's a gentleman, Madam—he wants to see you.

MRS. MANNINGHAM. Tell him to go, Elizabeth. He wants to see my husband. My husband's out.

ELIZABETH. No, Madam—he wants to see you. You must see him, Madam.

MRS. MANNINGHAM. Oh, leave me alone. Tell him to go away. I want to be left alone.

ELIZABETH. Madam, Madam. I don't know what's going on between you and the Master, but you've got to hold up, Madam. You've got to hold up.

MRS. MANNINGHAM. I am going out of my mind, Elizabeth. That's what's going on.

ELIZABETH. [*Leaning over back of settee with her arms around* MRS. MANNINGHAM.] Don't talk like that, Madam. You've got to be brave. You mustn't go on lying here in the dark, or your mind *will* go. You must see this gentleman. It's *you* he wants—not the Master. He's waiting to see you. Come, Madam, it'll take you out of yourself.

MRS. MANNINGHAM. Oh, my God—what new torment is this? I'm not in a fit state, I tell you.

ELIZABETH. [*Crosses to back of Center table.*] Come, Madam, I'll turn up the light. [*She does so. Then* ELIZABETH *picks up box of matches and crossing to the desk lamp, lights it.*] There. Now you'll be all right.

MRS. MANNINGHAM. Elizabeth! What have you done? I can't have anyone in. I'm not fit to be seen.

ELIZABETH. You look all right, Madam. You mustn't take on so. Now—I'll call him in. [*Goes to the door and can be heard calling "Will you come in, please, sir?"*]

[*The door is heard to SLAM.* MRS. MANNINGHAM *rises, half paralyzed, then runs over to the mirror above the mantelpiece and adjusts her hair. Stands with her back to the fireplace, waiting.* ELIZABETH *returns, holding back the door.* DETECTIVE ROUGH *enters. He is middle-aged—greying, short, wiry, active, brusque, friendly, over-bearing. He has a low warming chuckle and completely dominates the scene from the beginning.*]

ROUGH. Thank you— Ah—good evening. [*As he crosses down to Left end of settee.*] Mrs. Manningham. I believe— How are you, Mrs. Manningham? [*Chuckling, offers his hand.*]

MRS. MANNINGHAM. [*Shaking hands.*] How do you do? I'm very much afraid—

ROUGH. You're very much afraid you don't know me from Adam? That's about the root of the matter, isn't it?

[ELIZABETH *goes out Left Center, closing the doors.*]

MRS. MANNINGHAM. Oh, no—it's not that—but no doubt you have come to see my husband?

ROUGH. [*Who is still holding her hand, and looking at her appraisingly.*] Oh, no! You couldn't be further out.

[*Chuckling.*] On the contrary, I have chosen this precise moment to call when I knew your husband was out. May I take off my things and sit down? [*Starts to remove his coat.*]

MRS. MANNINGHAM. Why, yes, I suppose you may.

ROUGH. You're a good deal younger and more attractive than I thought, you know. But you're looking very pale. Have you been crying?

MRS. MANNINGHAM. Really—I'm afraid I don't understand at all.

ROUGH. You will do so, Madam, very shortly. [*Goes Left Center and begins to remove scarf.*] You're the lady who's going off her head, aren't you? [*Chuckles. To lower end of desk. He puts his hat on the desk and is removing his scarf and overcoat.*]

MRS. MANNINGHAM. [*Terrified.*] What made you say that? [*Goes toward him. Stops at Center.*] Who are you? What have you come to talk about?

ROUGH. Ah, you're running away with things, Mrs. Manningham, and asking me a good deal I can't answer at once. [*Taking off coat, and putting it on chair down Left and then crosses to down Left Center.*] Instead of that, I am going to ask you a question or two— Now, please, will you come here, and give me your hands? [*Pause. She obeys.*] Now, Mrs. Manningham, I want you to take a good look at me, and see if you are not looking at someone to whom you can give your trust. I am a perfect stranger to you, and you can read little in my face besides that. But I can read a great deal in yours.

MRS. MANNINGHAM. [*Pause.*] What? What can you read in mine?

ROUGH. Why, Madam, I can read the tokens of one who has travelled a very long way upon the path of sorrow and doubt—and will have, I fear, to travel a little further yet before she comes to the end. But I fancy she is coming towards the end, for all that. Come now, are you going to trust me, and listen to me?

MRS. MANNINGHAM. [*Pause.*] Who are you? God knows I need help.

ROUGH. [*Still holding her hands.*] I very much doubt whether God knows anything of the sort, Mrs. Manningham. If he did I believe he would have come to your aid before this. But I am here, and so you must give me your faith.

MRS. MANNINGHAM. [*Withdraws her hand and withdraws a step.*] Who are you? Are you a doctor?

ROUGH. Nothing so learned, Ma'am. Just a plain police detective.

MRS. MANNINGHAM. [*Shrinks away.*] Police detective?

ROUGH. Yes. Or was some years ago. [*Crossing to chair Left of table.*] At any rate, still detective enough to see that you've been interrupted in your tea. Couldn't you start again, and let me have a cup? [*He stands back of chair Left of table and holds it for her.*]

MRS. MANNINGHAM. Why, yes—yes. I will give you a cup. It only wants water. [*She begins to busy herself with hot water, cup, pot, etc., throughout the ensuing conversation.*]

ROUGH. [*Crosses around above table and to back of chair Right of it.*] You never heard of the celebrated Sergeant Rough, Madam? Sergeant Rough, who solved the Claudesley Diamond Case—Sergeant Rough, who hunted down the Camberwell dogs—Sergeant Rough, who brought Sandham himself to justice. [*He has his hand on back of chair, as he looks at her*] Or were all such sensations before your time?

MRS. MANNINGHAM. [*Looking up at* ROUGH.] Sandham? Why, yes—I have heard of Sandham—the murderer—the Throttler.

ROUGH. Yes—Madam—Sandham the Throttler. And you are now looking at the man who gave Sandham to the man who throttled him. And that was the common hangman. In fact, Mrs. Manningham—you have in front of you one who was quite a personage in his day —believe it or not.

MRS. MANNINGHAM. [*As she adds water to the tea.*] I quite believe it. Won't you sit down? I'm afraid it won't be very hot.

ROUGH. Thank you— [*Sitting.*] How long have you been married, Mrs. Manningham?

MRS. MANNINGHAM. [*Pouring tea.*] Five years—and a little.

ROUGH. Where have you lived during all that time, Mrs. Manningham? Not here, have you?

MRS. MANNINGHAM. [*Putting milk in his cup and passing it to him.*] No—first we went abroad—then we lived in Yorkshire, and then six months ago my husband bought this house.

ROUGH. You bought it?

MRS. MANNINGHAM. Yes. I had a bit of money. My husband thought this was an excellent investment.

ROUGH. [*Taking cup.*] You had a bit of money, eh? That's very good. And does your husband always leave you alone like this in the evenings?

MRS. MANNINGHAM. Yes. He goes to his club, I believe, and does business.

ROUGH. Oh, yes— [*He is stirring his tea, thoughtfully.*]

MRS. MANNINGHAM. Yes—

ROUGH. And does he give you a free run of the whole house while he's out?

MRS. MANNINGHAM. Yes— Well, no—not the top floor. Why do you ask?

ROUGH. Ah—not the top floor—

MRS. MANNINGHAM. No—no—will you have some sugar?

ROUGH. Thanks.

MRS. MANNINGHAM. [*Bending over eagerly to answer his questions.*] What were you saying?

ROUGH. [*As he takes sugar. Lightly and chuckling.*] Before I go any further, Mrs. Manningham, I must tell you there's a leakage in this household. You have a maid called Nancy?

MRS. MANNINGHAM. Yes—yes—

ROUGH. And Nancy walks out of an evening with a young man named Booker in my employ. I only live a few streets away from you, you know.

MRS. MANNINGHAM. Oh, yes?

ROUGH. [*With a chuckle.*] Well, there is hardly anything

which goes on in this house, which is not described in detail to Booker, and from that quarter it reaches me.

MRS. MANNINGHAM. I knew it! I knew she talked. Now I know it, she shall be dismissed.

ROUGH. Oh, no—no such retribution is going to overtake her at the moment, Mrs. Manningham. In fact, I fancy you are going to be heavily in debt to your maid, Nancy. If it were not for her indiscretions I should not be here now, should I?

MRS. MANNINGHAM. What do you mean? What is this mystery? You must not keep me in the dark. What is it?

ROUGH. I'm afraid I shall have to keep you in the dark for a little, Mrs. Manningham, as I am still quite far down in the dark myself. Can I have another lump of sugar in this?

MRS. MANNINGHAM. Yes. [*Passes bowl to him.*]

ROUGH. Thank you. [*Pause.*] We were talking about the top floor. [*Helping himself to several lumps.*] There is a bedroom above this, and above that again *is* the top floor? Is that right?

MRS. MANNINGHAM. Yes. But it's shut up. When we first took the house, my husband said we would not need the upstairs quarters—until there were children.

ROUGH. You've never been up to the top floor, Mrs. Manningham?

[*Pause.*]

MRS. MANNINGHAM. No one goes up **there.**

ROUGH. Not even a servant to dust?

MRS. MANNINGHAM. No

ROUGH. Rather funny?

MRS. MANNINGHAM. [*Pause.*] Funny? [*Pause.*] I don't know— [*But she does think so.*]

ROUGH. I think it is. Now, Mrs. Manningham, to ask a personal question. When did you first get the notion into your head that your reason was playing you tricks?

MRS. MANNINGHAM. [*About to drink her tea. Pause. Looks at* ROUGH *and then sets her cup down.*] How did you know?

ROUGH. Never mind how I know. When did it begin?

MRS. MANNINGHAM. I always had that dread. My mother died insane, when she was quite young. When she was my age. But only in the last six months, in this house— things began to happen—

ROUGH. Which are driving you mad with fear?

MRS. MANNINGHAM. [*Gasping.*] Yes. Which are driving me mad with fear.

ROUGH. Is it the house itself you fear, Mrs. Manningham?

MRS. MANNINGHAM. Yes. I suppose it is. I hate the house. I always did.

ROUGH. And has the top floor got anything to do with it?

MRS. MANNINGHAM. Yes, yes, it has. That's how all this dreadful horror began.

ROUGH. Ah—now you interest me beyond measure. Do tell me about the top floor.

MRS. MANNINGHAM. I don't know what to say. It all

sounds so incredible— It's when I'm alone at night. I get the idea that—somebody's walking about up there— [*Looking up.*] Up there— At night, when my husband's out— I hear noises, from my bedroom, but I'm too afraid to go up—

ROUGH. Have you told your husband about this?

MRS. MANNINGHAM. No. I'm afraid to. He gets angry. He says I imagine things which don't exist—

ROUGH. It never struck you, did it, that it might be your own husband walking about up there?

MRS. MANNINGHAM. Yes—that *is* what I thought—but I thought I must be mad. [*As she turns to* ROUGH.] Tell me how you know.

ROUGH. Why not tell me first how *you* knew, Mrs. Manningham.

MRS. MANNINGHAM [*She rises and goes toward fireplace.*] It's true, then! It's true. I knew it. I knew it! When he leaves this house he comes back. He comes back and walks up there above—up and down—up and down. [*Turns to fireplace.*] He comes back like a ghost. How does he get up there?

ROUGH. [*Rises, crosses to* MRS. MANNINGHAM.] That's what we're going to find out, Mrs. Manningham. But there are such commonplace resources as roofs and fire escapes, you know. Now please don't look so frightened. Your husband is no ghost, believe me, and you are very far from mad. [*Pause.*] Tell me now, what made you first think it was him?

MRS. MANNINGHAM. It was the light—the gas light—

It went down and it went up— [*Starts to cry.*] Oh, thank God I can tell this to someone at last. I don't know who you are, but I must tell you. [*Crosses to* ROUGH.]

ROUGH. [*Takes her hands.*] Now try to keep calm. You can tell me just as well sitting down, can't you? Won't you sit down? [*He moves back.*]

MRS. MANNINGHAM. Yes—yes. [*She sits down on Right end of settee.*]

ROUGH. [*Looks around.*] The light, did you say? Did you see a light from a window?

MRS. MANNINGHAM. No. In this house, I can tell everything by the light of the gas. You see the mantle there. Now it's burning full. But if an extra light went on in the kitchen or someone lit it in the bedroom then this one would sink down. It's the same all over the house.

ROUGH. Yes—yes—that's just a question of insufficient pressure, and it's the same in mine. But go on, please.

MRS. MANNINGHAM. [*Pause.*] Every night, after he goes out, I find myself waiting for something. Then all at once I look round the room and see that the light is slowly going down. Then I hear tapping sounds—persistent tapping sounds. At first I tried not to notice it, but after a time it began to get on my nerves. I would go all over the house to see if anyone had put on an extra light, but they never had. It's always at the same time—about ten minutes after he goes out. That's what gave me the idea that somehow *he* had come back and that it was *he* who was walking about up there. I go up to the bedroom but I daren't stay there because I hear noises overhead. I want to scream and run out of the house. I sit here for hours, terrified, waiting for him to come back, and I always know when he's coming, always. Suddenly the light goes up again and ten minutes afterwards I hear his key in the lock [*A look at Left Center doors.*] and he's back again.

ROUGH. [*Lightly—chuckling.*] How very strange, indeed. You know, Mrs. Manningham, you should have been a policeman.

MRS. MANNINGHAM. Are you laughing at me? Do you think I imagine everything, too?

ROUGH Oh. no! I was merely praising the keenness of your observation. I not only think you are right in your suppositions, I think you have made a very remarkable discovery, and one which may have very far-reaching consequences.

MRS. MANNINGHAM. Far-reaching? How?

ROUGH. Well, let's leave that for the moment. [*Moves closer to her.*] Tell me, that is not the only cause, is it, which has lately given you reason to doubt your sanity? [*Pause.*] Has anything else been happening? [*Pause.*] Don't be afraid to tell me.

MRS. MANNINGHAM. Yes, there are other things. I hardly dare speak of them. It has been going on for so long. This business of the gas has only brought it to a head. It seems that my mind and memory are beginning to play me tricks.

ROUGH. Tricks? What sort of tricks? When?

MRS. MANNINGHAM. Incessantly—but more and more of late. He gives me things to look after, and when he asks for them they are gone, and can never be found. Then he misses his rings, or his studs, and I will hunt the place for them, and he will find them lying hidden at the bottom of my work-box. Twice the door of that room [*Turning and looking at door up Right.*] was found locked with the key vanished. That was also found at the bottom of my box. Only today, before you came, that picture had been taken from the wall and hidden. [*He looks around at picture.*] Who could have done it but myself? I try to remember. [*He turns to her.*] I break my heart trying to remember. But I can't. Oh, and then there was that terrible business about the dog—

ROUGH. The dog?

MRS. MANNINGHAM. We have a little dog. A few weeks ago, it was found with its paw hurt.—He believes— Oh, God, how I tell you what he believes—that I had hurt the dog. He does not let the dog near me now. He keeps it in the kitchen and I am not allowed to see it! I begin to doubt, don't you see? I begin to believe I imagine everything. Perhaps I do. Are you here? Is this a dream, too? Who are you? [*Rises.*] I'm afraid they are going to lock me up.

ROUGH. Do you know, Mrs. Manningham, it has occurred to me that you'd be all the better for a little medicine.

MRS. MANNINGHAM. Medicine. Are you a doctor? You're not a doctor, are you?

ROUGH. [*Chuckling.*] No, I'm not a doctor, but that doesn't mean that a little medicine would do you any harm.

MRS. MANNINGHAM. But I have medicine. He makes me take it. It does me no good, and I hate it. How can medicine help a mind that's ill?

ROUGH. Oh—but mine's an exceptional medicine. I have some with me now. You must try it.

MRS. MANNINGHAM. What medicine is it?

ROUGH [*He rises and goes over Left.*] You shall sample it and see. [*At Center.*] You see, it has been employed by humanity, for several ages, for the purpose of the instantaneous removal of dark fears and doubts. That seems to fit you, doesn't it? [*Crosses to Left to coat then turns to her.*]

MRS. MANNINGHAM. The removal of doubt. How could a medicine effect that?

ROUGH. Ah—that we don't know. The fact remains that it does. Here we are. [*Produces what is obviously a bottle of whiskey, and crosses to Left of Center table.*] You see, it comes from Scotland. Now, Madam, have you such a thing handy as two glasses or a couple of cups?

MRS. MANNINGHAM. [*Crosses to Left end of settee.*] Why—are you having some, too?

ROUGH. Oh, yes. I am having some above all things. We could use these cups, if you like.

MRS. MANNINGHAM. No. [*She goes to secretary and brings out two glasses and crosses to Right of Center table.*] I will get two—

ROUGH. Ah—thank you—the very thing. Now we shan't be long.

MRS. MANNINGHAM. What is it? I so dislike medicine. What does it taste like?

ROUGH. Delicious! Something between ambrosia and

methylated spirits. Do you mean to say you've never tasted good Scotch whiskey, Mrs. Manningham?

MRS. MANNINGHAM. Whiskey? But I must not take whiskey. I can't do that!

ROUGH. [*Pouring it out.*] You underestimate your powers, Mrs. Manningham. You see, I don't want you thinking you can't trust your reason. This will give you faith in your reason like nothing else— Now for some water— All right this will do. [*Takes water from pitcher and pours it into the glasses.*] There! [*Hands glass to her.*] Tell me— [*Is pouring water into his own.*] Did you ever hear of the Cabman's Friend, Mrs. Manningham?

MRS. MANNINGHAM. The Cabman's Friend?

ROUGH. Yes. How nice to see you smile. Here's your very good health. [*Drinks.*] Go on— [*She drinks.*] There— Is it so nasty?

MRS. MANNINGHAM. No. I rather like it. My mother used to give us this as children when we had the fever.

ROUGH. Ah, then you're a hardened whiskey drinker. But you'll enjoy it better sitting down.

MRS. MANNINGHAM. Yes. [*Sitting down on chair below fireplace. He drinks.*] What were you saying? Who is the Cabman's Friend?

ROUGH. Ah. The Cabman's Friend. [*Crosses to her.*] You should ask me who *was* the Cabman's Friend, Mrs. Manningham, for she was an old lady who died many years ago. [*Pause, as he puts whiskey on mantelpiece.*]

MRS. MANNINGHAM. An old lady years ago? What has she to do with me?

ROUGH. A great deal, I fancy, [*Crosses to Right end of*

settee.] if you will follow me patiently. Her name was Barlow—Alice Barlow, and she was an old lady of great wealth, and decided eccentricities. In fact, her principal mania in life was the protection of cabmen. You may think that an extraordinary hobby, but in her odd way she did a lot of good. She provided these men with shelters, clothing, pensions, and so forth, and that was her little contribution to the sum of the world's happiness; or rather her little stand against the sum of the world's pain. There is a great deal of pain in this world, Mrs. Manningham, you know. [*Crosses to upper end of fireplace.*] Well, it was not my privilege to know her, but it was my duty, on just one occasion, to see her. [*Turns to her.*] That was when her throat was cut open, and she lay dead on the floor of her own house.

MRS. MANNINGHAM. Oh, how horrible! Do you mean she was murdered?

ROUGH. Yes. [*Crosses to Right end of settee.*] She was murdered. I was only a comparatively young officer at the time. It made an extremely horrible, in fact I may say lasting, impression on me. You see the murderer was never discovered but the motive was obvious enough. Her husband had left her the Barlow rubies, [*Crosses to Left end of settee.*] and it was well known that she kept them, without any proper precautions, in her bedroom on an upper floor. [*Turns to her.*] She lived alone except for a deaf servant in the basement. Well, for that she paid the penalty of her life.

MRS. MANNINGHAM. But I don't see—

ROUGH. There were some sensational features about the case. The man seemed to have got in at about ten at night, and stayed till dawn. Apart, presumably, from the famous rubies, there were only a few trinkets taken, but the whole house had been turned upside down. and in the upper room every single thing was flung about. or torn open. Even the cushions of the chairs were ripped up with his bloody knife, and the police decided that it must have been a revengeful maniac as well as a robber. I had other theories, but I was a nobody then, and not in charge of the case.

MRS. MANNINGHAM. What were your theories?

ROUGH. [*Crossing up Right.*] Well, it seemed to me, from all that I gathered here and there, that the old lady might have been an eccentric, but that she was by no means a fool. It seemed to me [*Crossing to back of settee.*] that she might have been one too clever for this man. We presume he killed her to silence her, but what then? What if she had *not* been so careless? [*Slowly crossing to her.*] What if she had got those jewels cunningly hidden away in some inconceivable place, in the walls, floored down, bricked in, maybe? What if the only person who could tell him where they were was lying dead on the floor? Would not that account, Mrs. Manningham, for all that strange confusion in which the place was found? [*Crossing back of settee to Center.*] Can't you picture him, Mrs. Manningham, searching through the night, ransacking the place, hour after hour, growing more and more desperate. until at last the dawn comes and he has to slink out into the pale street, the blood and wreckage of the night behind? [*Turns to her.*] And the deaf servant down in the basement sleeping like a log through it all.

MRS. MANNINGHAM. Oh, how horrible! How horrible indeed! And was the man never found?

ROUGH. No, Mrs. Manningham, the man was never found. Nor have the Barlow rubies ever come to light.

MRS. MANNINGHAM. Then perhaps he found them after all, and may be alive today.

ROUGH. I think he is almost certainly alive today, but I don't believe he found what he wanted. That is, if my theory is right.

MRS. MANNINGHAM. Then the jewels may still be where the old lady hid them?

ROUGH. Indeed, Mrs. Manningham, if my theory is right the jewels *must* still be where she hid them. The official conclusion was quite otherwise. The police, naturally and quite excusably, presumed that the murderer had got them, and there was no re-opening of matters in those days. Soon enough the public forgot about it. I almost forgot about it myself. But it would be funny, wouldn't it, Mrs. Manningham, if after all these years I should turn out to be right.

MRS. MANNINGHAM. Yes, yes, indeed. But what has this to do with me?

ROUGH. Ah, that is the whole question, Mrs. Manningham. What, indeed? What has the obscure murder of an old lady fifteen years ago to do with an attractive, though I am afraid at present, somewhat pale and wan young woman, who believes she is going out of her mind? Well, believe there is a link, however remote, wild and strange it may be, and that is why I am here.

MRS. MANNINGHAM. It's all so confusing. Won't you—

ROUGH. Do you conceive it possible, Mrs. Manningham, that that man might never have given up hope of one day getting at the treasure which lay there?

MRS. MANNINGHAM. Yes. Yes. Possibly. But how—

ROUGH. Can you conceive that he may have waited years —gone abroad, got married even, until at last his chance came to resume the search begun on that terrible night? [*Crossing down to her.*] You don't follow where I am leading at all, do you, Mrs. Manningham?

MRS. MANNINGHAM. Follow you? I think so.

ROUGH. You know, Mrs. Manningham, of the old theory that the criminal always returns to the scene of his crime.

MRS. MANNINGHAM. Yes?

ROUGH Ah, yes, but in this case there is something more than morbid compulsion— There is real treasure there to be unearthed if only he can search again, search methodically, without fear of interruption, without causing suspicion. And how would he do that? [*All at once she rises.*] Don't you think— What's the matter, Mrs. Manningham?

MRS. MANNINGHAM. [*As she looks at brackets and backs away to Right Center.*] Quiet! Be quiet! He has come back! Look at the light! It is going down! [*Pause as LIGHT sinks.*] Wait! There! [*Pause.*] He has come back, you see. [*As she looks up at ceiling.*] He is upstairs now.

ROUGH. Dear me, now. How very odd that is. How very odd, indeed.

MRS. MANNINGHAM. [*Whispering.*] He is in the house, I tell you. You must go. He will know you are here. You must go.

[*WARN CURTAIN*]

ROUGH. How dark it is. [*Crosses down to Right end of settee.*] You could hardly see to read.

MRS. MANNINGHAM. You must go. He is in the house. Please go.

ROUGH. [*Quickly coming to her and taking her arms in his hands.*] Quiet, Mrs. Manningham, quiet! You have got to keep your head. Don't you see my meaning, yet? Don't you understand that this was the house?

MRS. MANNINGHAM. House? What house?

ROUGH. The old woman's house, Mrs. Manningham— This house, here, these rooms, these walls. Fifteen years ago Alice Barlow lay dead on the floor in this room. Fifteen years ago the man who murdered her ransacked this house—below and above—but could not find what he sought. What if he is still searching, Mrs. Manningham? [*Indicating upstairs.*] What if he is up there— still searching? Now do you see why you must keep your head?

MRS. MANNINGHAM. But my husband, my husband is up there!

ROUGH. [*Drops her arms.*] Precisely that, Mrs. Manningham. Your husband. [*Going for her drink on mantelpiece.*] You see, I am afraid you are married to a tolerably dangerous gentleman. [*Takes second glass off mantel and crosses to her.*] Now drink this quickly, as we have a great deal to do.

[*He stands there, holding out glass to her. She remains motionless.*]

THE CURTAIN FALLS

ACT TWO

ACT TWO

No time has passed. MRS. MANNINGHAM *takes the whiskey from* ROUGH *in a mechanical way, and stares at him.*

MRS. MANNINGHAM. This house— How do you know this was the house?

ROUGH. Why, Ma'am, because I was on the case, and came here myself, that's all.

MRS. MANNINGHAM. The idea is mad. I have been married five years. How can you imagine my husband is— what you imagine he may be?

ROUGH. Mrs. Manningham—

MRS. MANNINGHAM. Yes?—

[*Pause.*]

ROUGH. When the police came into this place fifteen years ago, as you can understand there was a great deal of routine work to be done—interviewing of relatives and friends and so forth. Most of that was left to me.

MRS. MANNINGHAM. Well?—

ROUGH. Well, amongst all the acquaintances and relatives, nephews and nieces, etc., that I interviewed, there happened to be a young man of the name of Sydney Power. I suppose you have never heard that name at all, have you?

MRS. MANNINGHAM. Power?—

ROUGH. Yes, Sydney Power. It conveys nothing to you?

MRS. MANNINGHAM. Sydney Power. No—

ROUGH. Well, [*Crosses to Left of table and turns to* MRS. MANNINGHAM *and during the following speech pours himself out another drink.*] he was a kind of distant cousin, apparently much attached to the old lady, and even assisting her in her good works. The only thing was that I remembered his face. Well, I saw that face again just a few weeks ago. It took me a whole day to recollect where I had seen it before, but at last I remembered.

MRS. MANNINGHAM. Well—what of it? What if you did remember him?

ROUGH. It was not so much my remembering Mr. Sydney Power, Mrs. Manningham. What startled me was the lady on his arm and the locality in which I saw him.

MRS. MANNINGHAM. Oh—who was the lady on his arm?

ROUGH. *You* were the lady on his arm, Mrs. Manningham, [*Turning toward window and crossing up Center.*] and you were walking down this street.

MRS. MANNINGHAM. [*Crossing to Right of table.*] What are you saying? Do you mean you think my husband—my husband is this Mr. Power?

ROUGH. Well, not exactly, for if my theories are correct — [*He drinks.*]

MRS. MANNINGHAM. What are you saying? [*Sits.*] You stand there talking riddles. You are so cold. You are as heartless and cold as he is.

ROUGH. [*Coming down to Left of table.*] No, Mrs. Manningham, I am not cold, and I am not talking riddles. [*Puts his drink on table.*] I am just trying to preserve a cold [*Sits.*] and calculating tone, because you are up against the most awful moment in your life, and your whole future depends on what you are going to do in the next hour. Nothing less. You have got to *strike* for your freedom, and *strike* now, for the moment may not come again.

MRS. MANNINGHAM. Strike——

ROUGH. [*As he leans across table to her.*] You are not going out of your mind, Mrs. Manningham. [*Rises.*] You are slowly, methodically, systematically being *driven* out of your mind. And why? Because you are married to a criminal maniac who is afraid you are beginning to know too much——a criminal maniac who steals back to his own house at night, still searching for something he could not find fifteen years ago. Those are the facts, wild and incredible as they may seem. [*Crossing to table.*] His name is no more Manningham than mine is. He is Sydney Power and he murdered Alice Barlow in this house. Afterward he changed his name, and he has waited all these years, until he found it safe to acquire this house in a legal way. He then acquired the empty house next door. Every night, for the last few weeks, he has entered that house from the back, climbed up on to its roof and come into this house by the skylight. I know that because I have seen him do it. [*Crossing to back of settee.*] You have watched the gas-light, and without knowing it been aware of the same thing. [*Pause as he crosses up Center then down to chair Left of table.*] He is up there now. Why [*Crossing to Left Center.*] he should employ this mad, secretive, circuitous way of getting at what he wants, God Himself only knows. For the same reason perhaps, that he employs this mad, secretive, circuitous way of getting rid of you: that is, by slowly driving you mad and into a lunatic asylum.

MRS. MANNINGHAM. Why?

ROUGH. The fact that you had some money, enough to buy this house is part of it, I expect. For now that he's got that out of you he doesn't need you any longer. [*Crosses and sits Left of table.*] Thank God you are not married to him, and that I have come here to save you from the workings of his wicked mind.

MRS. MANNINGHAM. Not married?—Not married?—He married me.

ROUGH. I have no doubt he did, Mrs. Manningham. [*Rises and turns away to Left.*] Unfortunately, or rather fortunately, [*Turns to her.*] he contracted the same sort of union with another lady many years before he met you. Moreover the lady is still alive, and the English law has a highly exacting taste in monogamy. You see, I have been finding things out about Mr. Sydney Power. [*A look at the ceiling.*]

MRS. MANNINGHAM. Are you speaking the truth? [*Rises.*] My God—are you speaking the truth? Where is this wife now?

ROUGH. [*Crossing to Left Center.*] I'm afraid, she is the length of the world away—on the Continent of Australia to be precise, where I know for a fact he spent two years. Did you know that?

MRS. MANNINGHAM. No. [*Pause. She crosses to front of settee and faces fireplace.*] I—did—not—know—that.

ROUGH. Ah, yes. If only I could find her, things would be easier, and that's the whole root of the matter, Mrs. Manningham. [*Crossing to back of settee.*] So far I am only dealing in guesses and *half facts*. I have got to have evidence, and that is why I came to see you. *You have got to give me the evidence* or *help* me find it.

MRS. MANNINGHAM. [*Turning upstage and facing* ROUGH.] This is my husband. Don't you understand— this is my husband. He married me. Do you ask me to betray the man who married me?

ROUGH. By which you mean, of course, the man who has betrayed you into thinking that you are married to him— don't you?

MRS. MANNINGHAM. But I'm married to him. You must go. I must think this out. You must go. I must cling to the man I married. Mustn't I?

ROUGH. Indeed, cling to him by all means, but do not imagine you are the only piece of ivy, on the garden wall. You can cling to him if you desire, as his fancy women in the low resorts of the town cling to him. This is the sort of wall you have to cling to, Ma'am.

MRS. MANNINGHAM. [*Sits on settee.*] Women? What are you suggesting?

ROUGH. I'm not suggesting anything. I am only telling you what I have seen. He comes to life at night, this gentleman upstairs, in more ways than one. [*Crossing to Center.*] I have made it my business to follow him on some of his less serious excursions, and I can promise you he has a taste in *unemployed actresses* which he is at no pains to conceal.

MRS. MANNINGHAM. [*After pause.*] God in heaven!
—what *am* I to believe?

ROUGH. [*Crossing to Left end of settee.*] Mrs. Manningham, it is hard to take everything from you, but you are
no more tied to this man, you are under no more obliga-
tion to him than those wretched women in those places.
You must learn to be thankful for that.

MRS. MANNINGHAM. [*Pause.*] What do you want me to
do? What do you want?

ROUGH. [*Pause as he crosses down and sits.*] I want his
papers, Mrs. Manningham—his identity. There is some
clue somewhere in this house, and we have got to get at
it. [*Looking around the room.* ROUGH *has now completely
changed his tone.*] Where does he keep his papers?

MRS. MANNINGHAM. [*Rises.*] Papers? I know of no
papers. Unless his bureau—

ROUGH. [*Rises—crosses at Center around Left end of
settee and looks around room and to Right.*] Yes. His
bureau? His bureau?

MRS. MANNINGHAM. Yes. There. [*Points to desk Left.
As he crosses and is above table.*] But he keeps it always
locked. [*He stops at Left Center.*] I have never seen it
open.

ROUGH. Ah—he keeps it locked, does he?

MRS. MANNINGHAM. It is just his desk—his bureau—

ROUGH. [*Crosses Left above desk and around to back of
it.*] Very well. We will have a look inside.

MRS. MANNINGHAM. But it is locked. How can you, if it
is locked?

ROUGH. Oh—it doesn't look so very formidable. You know, Mrs. Manningham, one of the greatest regrets of my life is that fate never made me one of two things— one was a gardener, [*Going to overcoat, to fetch ring of keys and implements.*] the other a burglar—both quiet occupations, Mrs. Manningham. As for burgling I think, if I'd started young, and worked my way up, I should have been a genius. [*Crosses back to desk.*] Now let's have a look at this.

MRS. MANNINGHAM. [*Crossing to him at desk.*] But you must not touch this. He will know what you have done.

ROUGH. Come now, Ma'am. You're working with me, aren't you—not against me? [*Looks at desk.*] Yes— Yes— Now do you mind if I take off my coat? I'm a man who never feels at work until his coat's off. [*He is taking off his coat, and hanging on chair down Left, revealing a pink fancy shirt.*] Quite a saucy shirt, don't you think? You didn't suspect I was such a dandy, did you? Now. [*Sits at desk and gets out keys.*] Let's have a real look at this.

MRS. MANNINGHAM. [*After a pause. As she crosses up Center facing Right.*] But you must not tamper with that. He will know what you have done.

ROUGH. Not if we are clever enough. And this one here doesn't even ask for cleverness— You see, Mrs. Manningham, there are all manner of—

[*LIGHT comes up.*]

MRS. MANNINGHAM. [*She looks at brackets and crosses to above desk.*] Stop—stop talking— Haven't you noticed? Haven't you noticed something?

ROUGH. Noticed? I've only—

MRS. MANNINGHAM. Stop! Yes—I was right. Look. Can't you see? The light! It's going up. He's coming back.

ROUGH. The light?—

MRS. MANNINGHAM. Quiet! [*Pause, after which the light slowly goes up in a tense silence. Whispering.*] There. It's come back. You see. [*Crossing to Left Center.*] You must go. Don't you see? He's coming back— He's coming back and you must go!

ROUGH. [*Rises.*] God bless my soul. This looks as if the unexpected *has* entered in.

MRS. MANNINGHAM. Yes. He *always* does the unexpected. I never know what he'll do. You must go. [*Crosses to upper end of desk.*]

ROUGH. [*Without moving, looking up ruminatively.*] I wonder. Yes. Well, well— [*Puts the keys in his pocket and begins to put on his coat.*] Now—will you go and ring that bell for Elizabeth?

MRS. MANNINGHAM. Elizabeth. Why do you want her?

ROUGH. Do as I say, and ring the bell. At once. Please. Or you can go and fetch her if you like. [MRS. MANNINGHAM *crosses up and rings bell.*] Now let me see.

MRS. MANNINGHAM. Go, please!—Go, please do! You must go at once. [*Crossing to above desk.*] Why do you want Elizabeth?

ROUGH. [*Picks up overcoat, puts it on, then his scarf and crosses below desk to her.*] All in good time. He's not going to jump through the window, you know. In fact he can't be round at our front door in less than five minutes—unless he's a magician. Now can you see anything I've missed?

MRS. MANNINGHAM. No. No. [*Turns and sees whiskey bottle and crosses and gets it and gives it to* ROUGH.] Yes, the whiskey here.

ROUGH. Oh, yes. I told you you'd make a good policeman. Don't forget the glasses.

MRS. MANNINGHAM. Oh, do go, please, please go.

[ELIZABETH *enters Left Center.* MRS. MANNINGHAM *puts glasses away in secretary and slowly crosses down Right.*]

ROUGH. Ah—Elizabeth—come here will you?

ELIZABETH. [*Crosses to* ROUGH.] Yes, sir?

ROUGH. Elizabeth, you and I have got to do a little, quite calm, but rather quick thinking. You've told me you're anxious to help your mistress, Elizabeth?

ELIZABETH. Why, yes, sir, I told you I was, sir. But what's it all about?

ROUGH. Are you anxious to help your mistress, blindly, without asking any questions?

ELIZABETH. Yes, sir. But you see—

ROUGH. Come now, Elizabeth. Are you or are you not?

ELIZABETH. [*After pause, looking at* MRS. MANNINGHAM, *in quiet voice.*] Yes, sir.

ROUGH. Good. Now, Elizabeth, Mrs. Manningham and

I have reason to suppose that in about five minutes' time the master is returning to this house. He mustn't see me leaving. Would you be good enough to take me down to your kitchen and hide me away for a short space of time? You can put me in the oven if you like.

ELIZABETH. Yes, sir. But you see—

MRS. MANNINGHAM. [*As he crosses to window and looks out.*] You must go. You must go. He won't see you if you go now.

}[*Together*]

ROUGH. What were you saying, Elizabeth?

ELIZABETH. Yes, sir. You could come to the kitchen. But—Nancy's down there, sir.

ROUGH. Nancy! What the devil's this now? I thought this was Nancy's afternoon off. Was it not arranged that I should come when Nancy was away?

ELIZABETH. [*Agitated.*] Yes, sir. But for some reason she's stayed on. I think she's got a young man, and I couldn't make her go, could I, sir? If I'd done that, I'd've—

ROUGH. All right—all right. Then she was here when I came, and she knows I am here—is that it?

ELIZABETH. Oh, no— She was in the scullery when I answered the door, and I said it was a man who had come to the wrong house. She hasn't no idea, sir, and I'm—

ROUGH. All right. All right. [*Quickly crossing below the table to Right Center.*] That's better news. But it means you can't entertain me in the kitchen. [*At down Right*

Center turns to ELIZABETH.] Now where are you going to hide me, Elizabeth? Make up your mind quickly.

ELIZABETH. I don't know, sir. Unless you go to the bedroom. Mine and Nancy's, I mean.

ROUGH. [*Crossing up to Right of* ELIZABETH.] That sounds altogether entrancing! Shall we go there now?

ELIZABETH. [*Coming to him.* MRS. MANNINGHAM *goes Left.*] Yes, sir, but supposing Nancy went up there before she goes out?

ROUGH. You're a good soul and you think of everything, Elizabeth. [*Going to up Right Center.*] Where does this lead to, and what's the matter with this?

ELIZABETH. [*Crossing to* ROUGH.] It's where he dresses, where he keeps his clothes. Yes, sir. Go in there, sir. He won't see you there. There's a big wardrobe there, at the back.

ROUGH. [*Going toward up Right door.*] Excuse me. [*Goes through door up Right.*]

MRS. MANNINGHAM. [*Crossing to Center.*] Oh, Elizabeth.

ELIZABETH. [*Crosses to* MRS. MANNINGHAM.] It's all right, Ma'am. Don't take on so. It'll be all right.

MRS. MANNINGHAM. I'm sure he ought to go.

ELIZABETH. No, Ma'am. He knows best. [ROUGH *enters from up Right.*] He's bound to know best.

ROUGH. [*As he trots across to upper end of window for a peep.*] Perfect accommodation. [*Has seen something.*] Yes, there he is. [*Crossing to* MRS. MANNINGHAM.]

Now we really have got to hurry. Get off to bed, Mrs. Manningham, quick. And you, Elizabeth, go to your room. You can't get downstairs in time. Hurry, please. Elizabeth, turn down that lamp.

[ELIZABETH *does so. He goes to turn down gas.*]

MRS. MANNINGHAM. To bed? Am I to go to bed?

ROUGH. [*Really excited for the first time.*] Yes, quick. He's coming. Don't you understand? Go there and stay there. You have a bad headache—[*Cross to fireplace and start to turn down upper gas bracket.*]--a bad headache. [*Quite angry, turning from gas of downstage bracket.*] Will you go, in Heaven's name!

[MRS. MANNINGHAM *goes upstairs and* ELIZABETH *exits Left Center and to the Right leaving the doors open as* ROUGH *turns down the gas in the downstage bracket. There is a light from the hall through the open doors.* ROUGH *crosses to the Left end of the settee, pauses a moment watching the hall then nimbly on tip toes crosses up to the open doors and listens. After a short pause there is the sound of the front DOOR closing. He stiffens and starts to quietly trot to the up Right door and as he reaches up Right Center, feels his head, discovers his hat missing, and turning quickly trots to the desk, gets his hat, puts it on as he quickly crosses to up Right door and exits. There is a short pause and* MR. MANNINGHAM *appears in the doorway, peers into the room and enters, closes the doors and looks up the stairway, then crosses to upstage bracket turns it up, then to the downstage bracket and turns it up. Then he goes back of the settee, puts his hat on the settee, crosses to the bell and rings it. Then leisurely he starts to the fireplace. As he reaches the settee* ELIZABETH *opens the doors and enters.*]

ELIZABETH. Did you ring, sir?

MR. MANNINGHAM. [*Turning to* ELIZABETH.] Yes, I
did. [*Without yet saying why he has rung, he removes
his coat and places it over settee, and then comes and
stands with his back to the fireplace.*] Where is Mrs.
Manningham, Elizabeth?

ELIZABETH. I think she's gone to bed, sir. I think she had
a bad headache and went to bed.

MR. MANNINGHAM. Oh, indeed. And how long has she
been in bed, do you know?

ELIZABETH. She went just a little while ago, sir—I think,
sir—

MR. MANNINGHAM. Oh. I see. Then we must be quiet,
mustn't we? Walk about like cats.—Can you walk about
like a cat, Elizabeth?

ELIZABETH. [*Trying to smile.*] Yes, sir. I think so, sir.

MR. MANNINGHAM. [*Mincing upstage.*] Very well,
Elizabeth. Walk about like a cat. All right. That's all.

ELIZABETH. Yes, sir. Thank you, sir.

[*Just as* ELIZABETH *is going to exit, he calls her back.*]

MR. MANNINGHAM. Er—Elizabeth.

ELIZABETH. [*Coming back.*] Yes, sir? [MANNINGHAM
is again silent.] Did you call, sir?

MR. MANNINGHAM. Yes. Why haven't you cleared away
the tea things?

ELIZABETH. [*Crossing to above table.*] Oh—I'm sorry,
sir. I was really just about to, sir.

MR. MANNINGHAM. [*Crossing left to Left Center.*] Yes. I think you had better clear away the tea things, Elizabeth.

ELIZABETH. Yes, sir. [*After pause, putting a dish on the tray.*] Excuse me, sir, but were you going to have some supper, sir?

MR. MANNINGHAM. [*Crossing to desk.*] Oh, yes. I am going to have supper. The question is, am I going to have supper here?

ELIZABETH. Oh, yes, sir. Are you having it out, sir?

MR. MANNINGHAM. Yes, I am having it out. [MANNINGHAM *takes off his undercoat and puts it carefully over a chair Left of table. He is beginning to undo his tie.*] I have come back to change my linen.

[*He is undoing his collar. There is a pause.*]

ELIZABETH. [*Looks up and realizes his coat is off.*] Do you want a fresh collar, sir? Shall I get you a fresh collar?

MR. MANNINGHAM. Why, do you know where my collars are kept?

ELIZABETH. Why, yes, sir. In your room, there, sir. Shall I get you one, sir?

MR. MANNINGHAM. What a lot you know, Elizabeth. And do you know the sort of collar I want tonight?

ELIZABETH. Why yes, sir— I think I know the sort of collar, sir.

MR. MANNINGHAM. [*As he crosses up back of settee.*] Then all I can say is you know a great deal more than I do— No— I think you must let me choose my own collar— [*Turns to* ELIZABETH.] That is, if I have your permission, Elizabeth.

ELIZABETH. [*Gazing at him.*] Yes, sir—yes, sir—

[MANNINGHAM *crosses to door up Right and exits.* ELIZABETH *puts on the table the plate she is holding and lowers her head, remaining motionless in suspense. Not a sound comes from the other room, and nearly a quarter of a minute goes by. At last* MANNINGHAM *comes out in a perfectly leisurely way. He is putting his tie on and crosses down to mirror over fireplace, looking at himself in the mirror during the ensuing conversation.*]

MR. MANNINGHAM. What did you think about Mrs. Manningham tonight, Elizabeth?

ELIZABETH. Mrs. Manningham, sir? In what way do you mean, sir?

MR. MANNINGHAM. Oh—just as regards her general health, Elizabeth.

ELIZABETH. I don't know, sir. She certainly seems very unwell.

MR. MANNINGHAM. Yes. I doubt if you can guess to what extent she is unwell. [*Turns to* ELIZABETH.] Or are you beginning to guess?

ELIZABETH. I don't know, sir.

MR. MANNINGHAM. [*Crossing to back of settee.*] I'm afraid I was compelled to drag you and Nancy into our troubles tonight. Perhaps I should not have done that.

ELIZABETH. It all seems very sad, sir.

MR. MANNINGHAM. [*Smiling and somewhat appealingly as he takes a step toward* ELIZABETH.] I'm at my wits' end, Elizabeth. You know that, don't you?

ELIZABETH. I expect you are, sir.

MR. MANNINGHAM. I have tried everything. Kindness, patience, cunning—even harshness, to bring her to her senses. But nothing will stop these wild, wild hallucinations, nothing will stop these wicked pranks and tricks.

ELIZABETH. It seems very terrible, sir.

MR. MANNINGHAM. You don't know a quarter of it, Elizabeth. You only see what is forced upon your attention—as it was tonight. You have no conception of what goes on all the time. [*He is looking at his tie in his hand.*] No—not this one, I think— [*Starts to up Right door.*]

ELIZABETH. Do you want another tie, sir?

MR. MANNINGHAM. [*Stops and turns to* ELIZABETH.] Yes. [*He strolls again into the other room.* ELIZABETH *turns and watches the up Right door intently. After a pause, he comes out with another tie. As he enters* ELIZABETH *quickly turns to tea table. He crosses down to fireplace mirror. He is putting his tie on during the ensuing conversation.*] I suppose you know about Mrs. Manningham's mother, Elizabeth?

ELIZABETH. No, sir. What of her, sir?

MR. MANNINGHAM. Not of the manner in which she died?

ELIZABETH. No, sir.

MR. MANNINGHAM. She died in the mad-house, Elizabeth, without any brain at all in the end.

ELIZABETH Oh, sir!—How terrible, sir

MR. MANNINGHAM. Yes, terrible indeed. The doctors could do nothing. [*Pause. Turns to* ELIZABETH.] You know, don't you, that I shall have to bring a doctor to Mrs. Manningham before long, Elizabeth? [*As he crosses to Left below table and to Left of it and gets his undercoat.*] I have fought against it to the last, but it can't be kept a secret much longer.

ELIZABETH. No, sir— No. sir—

MR. MANNINGHAM. [*Putting on his undercoat.*] I mean to say, you know what goes on. You can testify to what goes on, can't you?

ELIZABETH Indeed, sir Yes.

MR. MANNINGHAM. Indeed, you may *have* to testify in the end. Do you realize that? [*Pause. Sharp.*] Eh?

ELIZABETH [*Looking quickly up at him.*] Yes, sir. I would only wish to help you both, sir.

MR. MANNINGHAM. [*Crossing below table to settee, gets coat and puts it on, crosses to mirror and adjusts coat.*] Yes, I believe you there, Elizabeth. You're a very good soul. I sometimes wonder how you put up with things in this household—this dark household. I wonder why you do not go. You're very loyal.

ELIZABETH. [*Looking at him in an extraordinary way. He cannot see her.*] Always loyal to you, sir. Always loyal to you.

MR. MANNINGHAM. There now, how touching. I thank you, Elizabeth. [*Crosses back of settee to* ELIZABETH.] You will be repaid later for what you have said, and repaid in more ways than one. You understand that, don't you?

ELIZABETH. Thank you, sir. I only want to serve, sir.

MR. MANNINGHAM. [*Crosses back of settee, gets hat.*] Yes, I know that. Well, Elizabeth, I am going out. In fact, I'm even going to try to be a little gay. Can you understand that, or do you think it is wrong?

ELIZABETH. Oh, no, sir. No. You should get all the pleasure you can, sir, while you can.

MR. MANNINGHAM. I wonder—yes—I wonder—it's a curious existence, isn't it— Well—good night, Elizabeth. [*Goes off Left Center and to Left.*]

ELIZABETH. Good night, sir—good night.

[MANNINGHAM *has left the door open.* ELIZABETH *quickly crosses up to door and looks after him. After a pause* ROUGH *comes forth and* ELIZABETH *turns to him. He and* ELIZABETH *stand there looking at each other. At last,* ROUGH *goes to the window and looks out. The* DOOR *is heard slamming.*]

ROUGH. [*Coming back to* ELIZABETH.] He was right when he said you would be repaid, Elizabeth. Though not in the way he thinks. [*Taking off hat, puts it on desk then his overcoat and muffler and puts them on chair down Left. Pause.*] Will you go and get Mrs. Manningham?

ELIZABETH. Yes, sir. I'll get her, sir. [*Starts to stairs.*]

[ROUGH *gets implements out of overcoat pocket.* MRS. MANNINGHAM *comes downstairs.*]

ROUGH. Ah—there you are.

MRS. MANNINGHAM. I saw him go.

[ELIZABETH *takes tray and exits Left Center to Right.*]

ROUGH. Now we must get back to work.

MRS. MANNINGHAM. What did he want? What did he come back for?

ROUGH. He only came to change his clothes. Turn up the lamp, will you? [MRS. MANNINGHAM *does so, and comes to him as he again reaches desk.*] Now let's have another look at this.

MRS. MANNINGHAM. [*Crosses to desk.*] What if he comes back again? There is no light to warn us now.

ROUGH. Oh, you've realized that, have you? Well, Mrs. Manningham, we've just got to take that risk. [*Takes his keys from pocket.*] This is going to be child's play, I fancy. Just a little patience—a little adroitness in the use— [*The front DOOR slams.*] What's that?—Go and have a look, will you? [MRS. MANNINGHAM *crosses to the window.*] We seem to be rather bothered this evening, don't we?

MRS. MANNINGHAM. It's all right. It's only Nancy. I forgot. She usually goes out at this time.

ROUGH. She uses the front door—does she?

MRS. MANNINGHAM. Oh, yes. Indeed she does. She behaves like the mistress in this house.

ROUGH. A saucy girl. [*The top of the bureau opens.*]

Ah—here we are. Next to a key there's nothing a lock appreciates like kindness.

MRS. MANNINGHAM. Will you be able to close it again?

ROUGH. Yes. No damage done. There we are. [*Pulls the upstage drawer out and puts it up on top of desk.* MRS. MANNINGHAM *turns away to Right.*] Now. Let's see. Doesn't seem much here. [*Picks up brooch.*] And when she got there the cupboard was bare—and so the poor detective—

MRS. MANNINGHAM. What is that in your hand? What is that in your hand?

ROUGH. [*Holding up a brooch.*] Why, do you recognize this?

MRS. MANNINGHAM. Yes! My brooch! Yes! Is there anything else there? What else is there?—Look, my watch! Oh, God, it's my watch!

ROUGH. This also is your property then? [*He is watching her.*]

MRS. MANNINGHAM. Yes. Both of them. This watch I lost a week ago—my brooch has been missing three months. And he said he would give me no more gifts because I lost them. He said that in my wickedness [*He looks in drawer.*] I hid them away! Inspector, is there anything else—? [*Pause. She crosses to upper end of the desk and looks over his shoulder.*] Is there a bill there? [*He looks up at her.*] Is there a grocery bill?

ROUGH. [*Searching drawer.*] A grocery bill?—No— There doesn't seem to be— [*He has pulled out a letter which he drops on the desk.*]

MRS. MANNINGHAM. [*Picking up letter.*] One moment— One moment— This letter!—this letter! [*She
goes on reading it.*] It's from my cousin—my cousin—

ROUGH. Is your husband's correspondence with your
relations very much to the point at the moment, Mrs.
Manningham?

MRS. MANNINGHAM. You don't understand. [*Speaking
rapidly.*] When I was married I was cast off by all my
relations. I have not seen any of them since I was married. They did not approve my choice. I have longed to
see them again more than anything in the world. When
we came to London—to this house, I wrote to them, I
wrote to them twice. There never was any answer. Now
I see why there never was any answer. [*Dazed.*] This letter is to me. It's from my cousin.

ROUGH. [*Cynically.*] Yet you never got it. Now you're
beginning to understand, Mrs. Manningham?

MRS. MANNINGHAM. [*As she crosses to chair Left of
table and sits.*] Listen. Let me read to you what he says.
Let me read it to you. [*Feverishly.*] "Dear Cousin—
All of us were overjoyed to hear from you again."
[*Looks up at* ROUGH.] Overjoyed, do you hear that?
[*Returns to reading the letters.*] He goes on to say that
his family are in Devonshire, and that they have gone to
the country. He says we must meet and recapture old
ties. [*She is showing signs of great emotion.*] He says
that they all want to see me—that I must go and stay
with them—that they will give me—that they will give
me their Devonshire cream to fatten my cheeks, and
their fresh air to bring the sparkle back to my eyes—
they will give me— They'll give me— [*Breaking down.*

ROUGH *crosses to her.*] Dear God, they wanted me back! They wanted me back all the time!—

ROUGH. [*Coming to her as she cries softly.*] Poor child. You shall have your Devonshire cream and you shall have the fresh air to bring the sparkle back into your eyes. [*She looks up at him.*] Why, I can see a sparkle in them already. If you will be brave now and trust me, you will not have to wait long. Are you going to trust me?

MRS. MANNINGHAM. Thank you, Inspector, for bringing me this letter. [ROUGH *crosses up and to back of desk.*] What do you wish me to do?

ROUGH. For the moment, nothing. Tell me. This drawer here. It seems to me to have a special lock. Has it ever been open to your knowledge?

MRS. MANNINGHAM. [*Hesitantly.*] No.

ROUGH. No?—I suspected as much. Yes, this is a tougher proposition, I'm afraid. [*He goes to his overcoat and produces an iron instrument.*]

MRS. MANNINGHAM. [*Rising and crossing to Center to stop him.*] What are you going to do? Are you going to force it?

ROUGH. [*Calmly.*] If I possibly can. I don't know that—

MRS. MANNINGHAM. [*Crossing to desk.*] But you must not do that. You must not. What shall I say when my husband comes back?

ROUGH. [*Ironically. Getting his jimmy from coat.*] I have no idea *what* you will say when he comes back, Mrs. Manningham. But then I have no idea what you will do, Mrs. Manningham, if I have no evidence to remove you from his loving care for good.

MRS. MANNINGHAM. [*Torn with doubts.*] Oh, God. I am afraid. What can I do?

ROUGH. [*Sharply.*] There is only one thing we *can* do —go ahead. If we go back now, we are lost. I am going to force it and gamble on finding something. Are you with me?

MRS. MANNINGHAM. [*Tormented as she studies him.*] But, don't you see— All right. Force it! Force it! But be quick. [*She turns away to up Right.*]

ROUGH. There's no hurry, madam. He's quite happy where he is— Now I don't like violent methods—of this sort—it makes me feel like a dentist— There— [*There's a sound of splitting wood.*] All over now— Now let's have a look.

MRS. MANNINGHAM. [*After pause in which she watches him. As he pulls out the drawer.*] Is there anything there? Is there anything there?

ROUGH. [*Looking at papers.*] No I don't see anything yet—I don't see anything. Wait a minute— No— No— What's this? [*As he picks up a bundle of papers.*] Mr. Manningham—Mr. Manningham—Mr. Manningham—

MRS. MANNINGHAM. Is there nothing?

ROUGH. No— Not a thing. We have lost our gamble, ma'am, I'm afraid.

MRS. MANNINGHAM. [*Frightened.*] Oh, dear me, what are we to do? What are we to do? [*Crosses to Center.*]

ROUGH. [*Crossing above the desk to her.*] Some rapid thinking at the moment. Don't have any fear, Mrs. Manningham, I've been in many a tighter corner than this. Let's get those things back to begin with, shall we? Give me the watch and the brooch. [*Takes watch and brooch*.] We must put them back where they were. [*Starts up back of desk*.]

MRS. MANNINGHAM. Yes—here they are.

ROUGH. Here on the right, was it not?

MRS. MANNINGHAM. Yes. There— That's right. There.

ROUGH. [*Holding up brooch*.] A nice piece of jewelry. When did he give you this?

MRS. MANNINGHAM. Soon after we were married. But it was only second hand.

ROUGH. Second hand, eh? I'm afraid you got everything second hand, from this gentleman, Mrs. Manningham. Well—that's all right. [*He puts brooch in drawer and drawer back in desk*.] Now I must lock this up again, [*Closes the second drawer*.] if I can— [*About to lock first drawer*.] Second hand did you say?—How did you know that brooch was second hand, Mrs. Manningham?

MRS. MANNINGHAM. There's an affectionate inscription to someone else inside.

ROUGH. [*Vaguely*.] Oh— Is there?—[*Opens first drawer*.] Why didn't you tell me that—

MRS. MANNINGHAM. Why—I only found it myself a little while ago.

ROUGH. [*As he takes out brooch*.] Oh—really. Do you know, I have a feeling I have seen this somewhere before? Where is this inscription you speak of?

MRS. MANNINGHAM. It is a sort of trick. I only discovered it by accident. You pull the pin at the back. It goes to the right, [*He follows directions.*] and then to the left. It opens out like a star.

ROUGH. [*Crossing to Center. As he opens it.*] Oh, yes— Yes— Ah—here we are. Yes. [*As he sits Left of table and takes out his jeweler's glass.*] How very odd. What are these spaces here?

MRS. MANNINGHAM. [*Crosses to Left Center.*] There were some beads in it, but they were all loose and falling out—so I took them out.

ROUGH. Oh—there were some beads in it, but they were all loose and falling out—so you took them out. [*Pause.*] Have you got them by any chance?

MRS. MANNINGHAM. Yes. [*Pause. He shows interest.*] I think so. I put them in a vase.

ROUGH. May I see them, please?

MRS. MANNINGHAM. Yes. [*Goes to mantelpiece. Crosses below settee. He rises and goes up back of table.*] They should still be here.

ROUGH. There should be nine altogether, I think.

MRS. MANNINGHAM. Yes, that's right, I think there were. Yes. [*Takes vase down from upper end of mantel.*] Here they are. Here are some of them at any rate.

ROUGH. [*Crossing to her.*] Let me see, will you?—Ah— Thank you. [*Gets the rubies and quietly crosses to back of table and puts rubies in the brooch.*] Try and find them all, will you? [*She goes back to mantel.*] Did you happen to read this inscription at any time, ma'am?

MRS. MANNINGHAM. Yes, I read it. Why?

ROUGH. [*Reading.*] "Beloved A.B. from C.B. Eighteen fifty-one." [*Looking up at her.*] Does nothing strike you about that?

MRS. MANNINGHAM. No. What of it? What should strike me?

ROUGH. Really, I should have thought that as simple as A.B.C. Have you got the others? There should be four more.

MRS. MANNINGHAM. [*Crossing back to him.*] Yes. Here they are.

ROUGH. Thank you. [*Takes them.*] That's the lot. [*He is putting them in brooch on the table.*] Now tell me this —have you ever been embraced by an elderly detective in his shirt sleeves?

MRS. MANNINGHAM. What do you mean?

ROUGH. For that is your immediate fate at the moment. [*Puts down brooch and comes to her.*] My dear Mrs. Manningham— [*Kisses her.*] My dear, dear Mrs. Manningham! [*Steps back from her and takes her hands.*] Don't you understand?

MRS. MANNINGHAM. No, what are you so excited about?

ROUGH. [*Leaves her, and picks up brooch.*] There, there you are, Mrs. Manningham. The Barlow rubies—complete. Twelve thousand pounds' worth before your very eyes! [*Crosses to her and gives her brooch.*] Take a good look at them before they go to the Queen.

MRS. MANNINGHAM. But it couldn't be—it couldn't.

They were in the vase all the time. [*She glances toward mantel, then back at him.*]

ROUGH. Don't you see? Don't you see the whole thing? *This* is where the old lady hid her treasure—in a common trinket she wore all the day. I knew I had seen this somewhere before. And where was that? [*Crossing to Left Center.*] In portraits of the old lady—when I was on the case. She wore it on her breast. I remember it clearly though it was fifteen years ago. Fifteen years! [*Crosses to* MRS. MANNINGHAM.] Dear God in Heaven, am I not a wonderful man!

MRS. MANNINGHAM. And I had it all the time. I had it all the time.

ROUGH. And all because he could not resist a little common theft along with the big game— Well, it is I who am after the big game now. [*He shows signs of going.*]

MRS. MANNINGHAM. [*Crosses to front of table.*] Are you going?

ROUGH. Oh, yes. I must certainly go. [*Begins to collect his coat and things.*] And very quickly at that.

MRS. MANNINGHAM. Where are you going? Are you going to leave me? What are you going to do?

ROUGH I am going to move Heaven and earth—Mrs. Manningham—and if I have any luck I— [*Looking at his watch.*] It's very early yet. What time do *you* think he'll be back?

MRS. MANNINGHAM. I don't know. He's not usually in till eleven.

ROUGH. Yes. So I thought. Let's hope so. That will give

me time. Here. give me that. Have you closed it? [*Takes brooch.*] We will put it back where we found it. [*He crosses above desk to upstage drawer.*]

MRS. MANNINGHAM. [*Follows to upper end of desk.*] But what are you going to do?

ROUGH. It's not exactly what I am going to do. It's what the Government is going to do in the person of Sir George Raglan. Yes, ma'am. Sir George Raglan. No one less. The power above all the powers that be. [*Puts brooch in drawer—closes and locks drawer.*] He knows I am here tonight, you see. But he didn't know I was going to find what I have found. [*Pause. Looks at broken drawer.*] Yes— We've done for that, I'm afraid— Well, we must just risk it, that's all. [*Tries to force broken drawer into place.*] Now, Mrs. Manningham, you will serve the ends of justice best by simply going to bed. [*Crosses to* MRS. MANNINGHAM.] Do you mind going to bed?

MRS. MANNINGHAM. No. I will go to bed. [*She starts upstairs.*]

[*WARN CURTAIN*]

ROUGH. Good. Go there and stay there. Your headache is worse. Remember be ill. Be anything. But stay there, you understand. I'll let myself out. [*Crosses up to Left Center door.*]

MRS. MANNINGHAM. [*Suddenly. Comes downstairs and crosses to* ROUGH.] Don't leave me. Please don't leave me. I have a feeling— Don't leave me.

ROUGH. Feeling? What feeling?

MRS. MANNINGHAM. A feeling that something will happen if you leave me. I'm afraid. I haven't the courage.

ROUGH. Have the goodness to stop making a fool of yourself, Mrs. Manningham. Here's your courage. [*He gives her whiskey, taking it from pocket.*] Take some more of it, but don't get tipsy and don't leave it about. [*Pause—crosses up to doors.*] Good-bye. [*He is at Left Center doors, opens them and is about to exit.*]

MRS. MANNINGHAM. Inspector.

ROUGH. [*Turns to her.*] Yes.

MRS. MANNINGHAM. [*Summoning courage.*] All right. Good-bye. [*She starts up the stairs.*]

ROUGH. [*Pause. As he exits.*] Good-bye. [*Shuts the door. Pause as she stops on the stairs and glances around the room.* ROUGH *suddenly opens the door.*] Mrs. Manningham!

MRS. MANNINGHAM. Yes.

[ROUGH *motions to her to go upstairs. She does so and he watches her.*]

ROUGH. Good-bye.

[*When she is out of sight around the curve on the stairs he exits and closes the doors.*]

THE CURTAIN FALLS

ACT THREE

ACT THREE

The time is eleven the same night. The room is in dark-
ness, but the Left Center door is open and a dim light in
the passage outside can be seen. There is the sound of the
front DOOR shutting. FOOTSTEPS can be heard, and
MANNINGHAM appears outside. He stops to turn out the
light in the passage. He enters the room and goes to the
lamp on the Center table and turns it up. Then he lights
the two brackets and crosses to table up Right and puts
his hat on it. He goes in a slow and deliberate way over
to the bell-cord and pulls it. He is humming to himself as
he goes over to the fireplace.
NANCY puts her head round the Left Center door. She
has only just come in and is dressed for out-of-doors.

NANCY. Yes, sir. Did you ring, sir?

MR. MANNINGHAM. Yes, Nancy, I did ring. It seems
that the entire household has gone to bed without leaving me my milk and without leaving me my biscuits.

NANCY. Oh, I'm sorry, sir. They're only just outside.
I'll bring them in! [*Turns to door then stops and turns*
to MR. MANNINGHAM.] Mrs. Manningham usually gets
them, doesn't she, sir? Cook's in bed and I've only just
come in.

MR. MANNINGHAM. Quite Nancy. Then perhaps you
will deputize for Mrs. Manningham, and bring them
into the room.

NANCY. Certainly, sir.

MR. MANNINGHAM. And after you do that, [*She stops in doorway.*] Nancy, will you go upstairs and tell Mrs. Manningham that I wish to see her down here.

NANCY. Yes, sir. Certainly, sir. [*Exits Left Center and turns to Right.*]

[MR. MANNINGHAM *walks into room up Right.* NANCY *returns. She has milk in a jug, a glass and biscuits on a tray, and puts them on the table. She goes upstairs. He enters from room up Right crosses slowly to above table then over to desk.* NANCY *comes downstairs and stops at the foot of the stairs.*]

MR. MANNINGHAM. Well, Nancy?

NANCY. She says she has a headache, sir, and is trying to sleep.

MR. MANNINGHAM. Oh—she still has a headache, has she?

NANCY. Yes, sir. Is there anything else you want, sir?

MR. MANNINGHAM. Did you ever know a time when Mrs. Manningham did not have a headache, Nancy?

NANCY No, sir. Hardly ever, sir.

MR. MANNINGHAM. [*Turns to* NANCY.] Do you usually perform your domestic tasks in outdoor costume, Nancy?

NANCY. I told you, sir. I've only just come in, and I heard the bell by chance.

MR. MANNINGHAM. Yes, that's just the point.

NANCY. How do you mean, sir?

MR. MANNINGHAM. Will you be so good as to come closer, Nancy, where I can see you. [NANCY *comes down stage a step. They look at each other in a rather strange way.*] Have you any idea of the time of the day, or rather night, Nancy?

NANCY. Yes, sir. It's a little after eleven, sir.

MR. MANNINGHAM. Are you aware that you came in half a minute, or even less, before myself?

NANCY. Yes, sir. I thought I saw you, sir.

MR. MANNINGHAM. Oh—you thought you saw me. Well, I certainly saw you.

NANCY. [*Looking away.*] Did you, sir?

MR. MANNINGHAM. Have you ever reflected, Nancy, that you are given a great deal of latitude in this house?

NANCY. I don't know, sir. I don't know what latitude means.

MR. MANNINGHAM. Latitude, Nancy, means considerable liberty—liberty to the extent of two nights off a week.

NANCY. [*Pause.*] Yes, sir.

MR. MANNINGHAM. Well, that's all very well. It is not so well, however, when you return as late as the master of the house. We ought to keep up some pretences, you know.

NANCY. Yes, sir. We must. [*She makes to go.*]

MR. MANNINGHAM. Nancy.

NANCY. [*Stops.*] Yes, sir?

MR. MANNINGHAM. [*In a more human tone.*] Where the devil have you been tonight, anyway?

NANCY. [*Pause—turns to him.*] Only with some friends, sir.

MR. MANNINGHAM. You know, Nancy, when you say friends, I have an extraordinary idea that you mean gentlemen friends.

NANCY. [*Looking at him.*] Well, sir, possibly I might.

MR. MANNINGHAM. You know, gentlemen friends have been known to take decided liberties with young ladies like yourself. Are you alive to such a possibility?

NANCY. Oh, no, sir. Not with me. I can look after myself.

MR. MANNINGHAM. Are you always so anxious to look after yourself?

NANCY. No, sir, not always, perhaps.

MR. MANNINGHAM. You know, Nancy, pretty as your bonnet is, it is not anything near so pretty as your hair beneath it. Won't you take it off and let me see it?

NANCY. [*As she removes hat and crosses to Right of chair Right of table.*] Very good, sir. It comes off easy enough. There— Is there anything more you want, sir?

MR. MANNINGHAM. Yes. Possibly. Come here, will you, Nancy?

NANCY. [*Pause.*] Yes, sir— [*Drops hat on chair Right of table. Coming to him.*] Is there anything you want, sir?—[*Changing tone as he puts his arms on her shoulders.*] What do you want?—eh— What do you want?

[MANNINGHAM *kisses* NANCY *in a violent and pro-longed manner. There is a pause in which she looks at him, and then she kisses him as violently.*] There! Can she do that for you? Can she do that?

MR. MANNINGHAM. Who can you be talking about, Nancy?

NANCY. You know who I mean all right.

MR. MANNINGHAM. You know, Nancy, you are a very remarkable girl in many respects. I believe you are jealous of your mistress.

NANCY. She? She's a poor thing. There's no need to be jealous of her. You want to kiss me again, don't you? Don't you want to kiss me? [MR. MANNINGHAM *kisses* NANCY.] There! That's better than a sick headache—ain't it—a sick headache and a pale face all the day.

MR. MANNINGHAM. Why yes, Nancy, I believe it is. I think, however, don't you, that it would be better if you and I met one evening in different surroundings.

NANCY. Yes. Where? I'll meet you when you like. You're mine now—ain't you—'cos you want me. You want me —don't you?

MR. MANNINGHAM. And what of you, Nancy. Do you want me?

NANCY. Oh, yes! I always wanted you, ever since I first clapped eyes on you. I wanted you more than all of them.

MR. MANNINGHAM. Oh—there are plenty of others?

NANCY. Oh, yes—there's plenty of others.

MR. MANNINGHAM. So I rather imagined. And only nineteen.

NANCY. Where can we meet? Where do you want us to meet?

MR. MANNINGHAM. [*Slowly crossing to front of settee and facing fireplace.*] Really, Nancy, you have taken me a little by surprise. I'll let you know tomorrow.

NANCY. [*Crossing to front of table.*] How'll you let me know, when she's about?

MR. MANNINGHAM. [*Quietly, half turning to* NANCY.] Oh, I'll find a way, Nancy, I don't believe Mrs. Manningham will be here tomorrow.

NANCY. Oh? Not that I care about her. [*Crossing to him.*] I'd like to kiss you under her very nose. That's what I'd like to do.

MR. MANNINGHAM. All right, Nancy. Now you had better go. I have some work to do.

NANCY. Go? I don't want to go.

MR. MANNINGHAM. [*Turns away from her.*] There, run along. I have some work to do.

NANCY. Work? What are you going to work at? What are you going to do?

MR. MANNINGHAM. [*Turns to* NANCY.] Oh—I'm going to write some letters. Then I— Go along, Nancy, that's a good girl.

NANCY. Oh, very well, sir. You shall be master for a little more. [*Her arms around his neck. Kisses him.*] Good night, your lordship [*Starts to door Left Center and picks up her hat on the way.*]

MR. MANNINGHAM. Good night.

NANCY. [*At door stops and turns to him.*] When shall you let me know tomorrow?

MR. MANNINGHAM. When I find time, Nancy, when I find time. Good night.

NANCY. Good night! [*Goes out into the hall Left Center—closes doors.*]

[MANNINGHAM *crosses above settee to back of desk and sits down. He rises and crosses to the secretary, gets some papers, crosses back to the desk and sits down again. He takes up the pen and begins to write. He stops and takes out his key ring which is on the other end of his watch chain and unlocks the upstage drawer, then turns to unlock the downstage drawer. He stops as he discovers it has been forced and quickly rises. He turns to the upstage drawer, opens it and rummages through it. He then looks toward the stairs, crosses below the desk and stops at up Left Center, turns and goes to the bell rope, pulls it and goes back of desk and takes a quick look at both drawers then closes them.*]

NANCY. [*Re-enters.*] Yes? What is it now?

MR. MANNINGHAM. Nancy, will you please go upstairs and take a message for me to Mrs. Manningham.

NANCY. Yes. What do you want me to say?

MR. MANNINGHAM. Will you please tell her that she is to come down here this instant, whether she is suffering from a sick headache or any other form of ailment.

NANCY. Just like that, sir?

MR. MANNINGHAM. Just like that, Nancy.

NANCY. With the greatest of pleasure, sir. [*Goes upstairs.*]

[MANNINGHAM *looks at the drawer again carefully. He walks over to the fireplace and stands with his back to it, waiting.*]

NANCY. [*Returns. On the bottom step.*] She won't come. She doesn't mean to come.

MR. MANNINGHAM. [*Steps forward.*] What do you mean, Nancy—she won't come?

NANCY. She said she can't come—she's not well enough. She's just shamming, if you ask me.

MR. MANNINGHAM. Really? Then she forces me to be undignified. [*Walking over the stairs.*] All right, Nancy, leave it to me.

NANCY. The door's locked. She's got it locked. I tried it.

MR. MANNINGHAM. Oh—really—the door is locked. is it? Very well— [*He starts up the stairs past her to the fifth step.*]

NANCY. She won't let you in. I can tell by her voice. She's got it locked and she won't open it. Are you going to batter it in?

MR. MANNINGHAM. [*Turns, comes down to* NANCY.] No—perhaps you are right, Nancy—[*Crosses above desk to chair. Sits and starts to write.*]—let us try more delicate means of attaining our ends— Perhaps you will take a note to this wretched imbecile and slip it under her door.

NANCY. Yes, I'll do that. [*Coming to desk.*] What are you going to write?

MR. MANNINGHAM. Never mind what I am going to write. I'll tell you what you can do though, Nancy.

NANCY. Yes? What?

MR. MANNINGHAM. Just go down to the basement and bring the little dog here, will you?

NANCY. [*Starts out, stops and turns.*] The dog?

MR. MANNINGHAM. The dog, yes.

NANCY. What's the game? What's the idea with the dog?

MR. MANNINGHAM. Never mind. Just go and get it, will you?

NANCY. [*Starts to Left Center door.*] All right.

MR. MANNINGHAM. Or on second thought perhaps you need not get the dog. [*She stops. Turns to him.*] We will just let it be supposed we have the dog. That will be even more delicate still. Here you are, Nancy. [*She crosses to desk.*] Please go and put this under the door.

NANCY. [*Pause.*] What's the idea? What have you written in this?

MR. MANNINGHAM. Nothing very much. Just a little smoke for getting rats out of holes. There. Run along.

NANCY. You're a rum beggar, ain't you? [*At stairs.*] Can't I look?

MR. MANNINGHAM. Go on, Nancy.

[NANCY *goes up. Left alone,* MANNINGHAM *shuts and locks the top of his desk. Then he comes down and carefully places an armchair facing the fireplace—as though he is staging some ceremony. He looks around the room. Then he takes up his place in front of the fire, and waits.* NANCY *comes downstairs.*]

NANCY. She's coming. It's done the trick all right.

MR. MANNINGHAM. Ah—so I thought. Very well, Nancy
Now I shall be obliged if you will go to bed at once.

NANCY. Go on. What's the game? What's the row
about?

MR. MANNINGHAM. Nancy, will you please go to bed?

NANCY. [*Coming forward, to him.*] All right, I'm going. [*Crosses to him, her arms around him. Kisses him.*]
Good night, old dear. Give her what-for, won't you.

MR. MANNINGHAM. Good night, Nancy.

NANCY. Ta-ta.

[MRS. MANNINGHAM *appears and stands on the stairs.*
MRS. MANNINGHAM *says nothing.* NANCY *goes out Left
Center and leaves door ajar. After a long pause,* MAN-
NINGHAM *goes to the door, and looks to see that* NANCY
*is not there, closes it He comes back and standing again
with his back to the fireplace, looks at her.*]

MR. MANNINGHAM. Come and sit down in this chair,
please, Bella.

MRS. MANNINGHAM. [*Unmoving.*] Where is the dog?
Where have you got the dog?

MR. MANNINGHAM. Dog? What dog?

MRS. MANNINGHAM. You said you had the dog. Have
you hurt it? Let me have it. Where is it? Have you hurt
it again?

MR. MANNINGHAM. Again? This is strange talk, Bella
—from you—after what you did to the dog a few weeks
ago. Come and sit down here.

MRS. MANNINGHAM. I do not want to speak to you. I am not well. I thought you had the dog and were going —to hurt it. That is why I came down.

MR. MANNINGHAM. The dog, my dear Bella, was merely a ruse to compel you to pay me a visit quietly. Come and sit down where I told you.

MRS. MANNINGHAM. [*Starts upstairs.*] No. I want to go.

MR. MANNINGHAM. [*Shouting.*] *Come and sit down where I told you!*

MRS. MANNINGHAM. [*Coming downstage to back of table.*] Yes—yes—what do you want?

MR. MANNINGHAM. Quite a good deal, Bella. Sit down and make yourself comfortable. We have plenty of time

MRS. MANNINGHAM. [*As she crosses back toward stairs.*] I want to go. You cannot keep me here. I want to go.

MR. MANNINGHAM. [*Calmly.*] Sit down and make yourself comfortable, Bella. We have plenty of time.

MRS. MANNINGHAM. [*Going to chair Left of table Center which he did not indicate and which is nearer the door and sits.*] Say what you have to say.

MR. MANNINGHAM. Now you are not sitting in the chair I indicated, Bella.

MRS. MANNINGHAM. What have you to say?

MR. MANNINGHAM. I have to say that you are not sitting in the chair I indicated. Are you afraid of me that you desire to get so near the door?

MRS. MANNINGHAM. No, I am not afraid of you.

MR. MANNINGHAM. No? Then you have a good deal of courage, my dear. However, will you now sit down where I told you?

MRS. MANNINGHAM. [*Rises slowly and crosses below table.*] Yes.

[*Pause.*]

MR. MANNINGHAM. [*As she crosses.*] Do you know what you remind me of, Bella, as you walk across the room?

MRS. MANNINGHAM. [*At Left end of settee—stops.*] No. What do I remind you of?

MR. MANNINGHAM. A somnambulist, Bella. Have you ever seen such a person?

MRS. MANNINGHAM. [*A step toward him.*] No, I have never seen one.

MR. MANNINGHAM. Haven't you? Not that funny, glazed, dazed look of the wandering mind—the body that acts without the soul to guide it? I have often thought you had that look, but it's never been so strong as tonight.

MRS. MANNINGHAM. [*Crosses to Right chair.*] My mind is not wandering.

MR. MANNINGHAM. No?—When I came in, Bella, I was told that you had gone to bed.

MRS. MANNINGHAM. Yes. I had gone to bed.

MR. MANNINGHAM. Then may I ask why you are still

fully dressed? [*She does not answer*.] Did you hear what I said?

MRS. MANNINGHAM. Yes, I heard what you said.

MR. MANNINGHAM. Then will you tell me why, since you had gone to bed, you are still fully dressed?

MRS. MANNINGHAM. I don't know.

MR. MANNINGHAM. You don't know? Do you know anything about anything you do?

MRS. MANNINGHAM. I don't know. I forgot to undress.

MR. MANNINGHAM. You forgot to undress. A curious oversight, if I may say so, Bella. [*Leaning over her*.] You know, you give me the appearance of having had a rather exciting time since I last saw you. Almost as though you have been up to something. Have you been up to anything?

MRS. MANNINGHAM. No. I don't know what you mean.

MR. MANNINGHAM. [*Straightens up*.] Did you find that bill I told you to find?

MRS. MANNINGHAM. No

MR. MANNINGHAM. [*Goes to milk on table*.] Do you remember what I said would happen to you if you did not find that bill when I returned tonight?

MRS. MANNINGHAM. No.

MR. MANNINGHAM. No? [*Is pouring milk into glass*.] No? [*She refuses to answer*.] Am I married to a dumb woman, Bella, in addition to all else? The array of your physical and mental deficiencies is growing almost overwhelming. I advise you to answer me.

MRS. MANNINGHAM. What do you want me to say?

MR. MANNINGHAM. I asked you if you remembered something. [*Going back to fireplace with glass of milk.*] Go on, Bella—what was it I asked you if you remembered?

MRS. MANNINGHAM. I don't understand your words. You talk round and round. My head is going round and round.

MR. MANNINGHAM. [*At fireplace.*] It is not necessary for you to tell me, Bella. I am just wondering if it might interrupt its gyratory motion for a fraction of a second, and concentrate upon the present conversation. [*Sips milk.*] And please, what was it I a moment ago asked you if you remembered?

MRS. MANNINGHAM. [*Laboured.*] You asked me if I remembered what you said would happen to me if I did not find that bill.

MR. MANNINGHAM. Admirable, my dear Bella! Admirable! We shall make a great logician of you yet—a Socrates—a John Stuart Mill! You shall go down to history as the shining mind of your day. That is, if your present history does not altogether submerge you—take you away from your fellow creatures. And there is a danger of that, you know, in more ways than one. [*Milk on mantel.*] Well—what did I say I would do if you did not find that bill?

MRS. MANNINGHAM. [*Choked.*] You said you would lock me up.

MR. MANNINGHAM. Yes. And do you believe me to be a man of my word? [*Pause in which she does not answer.*

Crossing back of settee to Center.] You see Bella, in a life of considerable and varied experience I have hammered out a few principles of action. In fact, I actually fancy I know how to deal with my fellowmen. I learned it quite early actually—at school in fact. There, you know, there were two ways of getting at what you wanted. One was along an intellectual plane, the other along the physical. If one failed one used the other. I took that lesson into life with me. Hitherto, with you, I have worked with what forbearance and patience I leave you to judge, along the intellectual plane. [*Crosses down and over to her.*] The time has come now, I believe, to work along the other as well— You will understand that I am a man of some power— [*She suddenly looks at him.*] Why do you look at me, Bella? I said I am a man of some power and determination, and as fully capable in one direction as in the other.—I will leave your imagination to work on what I mean.—However, we are really digressing— [*Starts to Left crossing back of table.*] You did not find the bill I told you to find.

MRS. MANNINGHAM. No.

MR. MANNINGHAM. Did you look for it? [*He moves toward desk.*]

MRS. MANNINGHAM. Yes.

MR. MANNINGHAM. Where did you look for it?

MRS. MANNINGHAM. Oh, around the room—

MR. MANNINGHAM. Around the room. Where around the room? [*Pause. At desk. As he bangs on the desk with his right hand.*] In my desk, for instance?

MRS. MANNINGHAM. No—not in your desk.

MR. MANNINGHAM. Why not in my desk?

MRS. MANNINGHAM. Your desk is locked.

MR. MANNINGHAM. Do you imagine you can lie to me?

MRS. MANNINGHAM. I am not lying.

MR. MANNINGHAM. [*Crosses to Center of desk.*] Come here, Bella.

MRS. MANNINGHAM. [*Coming to him.*] What do you want?

MR. MANNINGHAM. [*Pause.*] Now, listen to me. Your dark, confused, rambling mind has led you into playing some pretty tricks tonight—has it not?

MRS. MANNINGHAM. My mind is tired. [*She starts to stairs.*] I want to go to bed.

MR. MANNINGHAM. Your mind indeed is tired. Your mind is so tired that it can no longer work at all. You do not think. You dream. [*He slowly starts toward her.*] Dream all day long. Dream everything. Dream maliciously and incessantly. Don't you know that by now? [*She starts to give way.*] You sleep-walking imbecile, what have you been dreaming tonight—where has your mind wandered—that you have split [*Pounds on desk.*] open my desk? What strange diseased dream have you had tonight—eh?

MRS. MANNINGHAM. Dream? Are you saying I have dreamed— Dreamed all that happened?—

MR. MANNINGHAM. All that happened when, Bella? To-night? Of course you dreamed all that happened—or rather all that didn't happen.

MRS. MANNINGHAM. Dream— Tonight—are you saying I have dreamed? [*Pause.*] Oh, God—have I dreamed? Have I dreamed again?—

MR. MANNINGHAM. Have I not told you—?

MRS. MANNINGHAM. [*Storming.*] I haven't dreamed. I haven't. Don't tell me I have dreamed. In the name of God don't tell me that!

MR. MANNINGHAM. [*Speaking at the same time, and forcing her down into small chair Left.*] Sit down and be quiet. Sit down! [*More quietly and curiously.*] What was this dream of yours, Bella? You interest me.

MRS. MANNINGHAM. I dreamt of a man— [*Hysterical.*] I dreamt of a man—

MR. MANNINGHAM. [*Now very curious.*] You dreamed of a man, Bella? What man did you dream of, pray?

MRS. MANNINGHAM. A man. A man that came to see me. Let me rest! Let me rest!

MR. MANNINGHAM. Pull yourself together, Bella. What man are you talking about?

MRS. MANNINGHAM. I dreamed a man came in here.

MR. MANNINGHAM. [*As he grasps her neck and slowly raises her.*] I know you dreamed it, you gibbering wretch! I want to know more about this man of whom you dreamed. Do you hear! Do you hear me?

MRS. MANNINGHAM. I dreamed—I dreamed—

[*She looks off at door up Right, transfixed.* MANNINGHAM *turns and looks as* ROUGH *enters door up Right.*

MANNINGHAM *releases her and she sinks back into the chair.*]

ROUGH. [*As he crosses to chair Right of table.*] Was I any part of this curious dream of yours, Mrs. Manningham?—Perhaps my presence here will help you to recall it.

MR. MANNINGHAM. [*After pause. Crossing to Left Center.*] May I ask who the devil you are, and how you got in?

ROUGH. [*Crosses back of chair.*] Well, who I am seems a little doubtful. Apparently I am a mere figment of Mrs. Manningham's imagination. As for how I got in, I came in, or rather I came back—or better still, I effected an entrance a few minutes before you, and I have been hidden away ever since.

MR. MANNINGHAM. And would you be kind enough to tell me what you are doing here?

ROUGH. [*Hands on chair back.*] Waiting for some friends, Mr. Manningham, waiting for some friends. Don't you think you had better go up to bed, Mrs. Manningham? You look very tired.

MR. MANNINGHAM. Don't you think you had better explain your business, sir?

ROUGH. Well, as a mere figment, as a mere ghost existing only in your wife's mind, I can hardly be said to have any business. Tell me, Mr. Manningham, can you see me? [*Spreading his hands as he makes a complete turn.*] No doubt your wife can, but it must be difficult for you. Perhaps if she goes to her room I will vanish, and you won't be bothered by me any more.

MR. MANNINGHAM. Bella. Go to your room. [*She rises, staring at* BOTH *in turn in apprehension and wonderment, goes to the stairs.*] I shall find out the meaning of this, and deal with you in due course.

MRS. MANNINGHAM. I—

MR. MANNINGHAM. Go to your room. I will call you down later. I have not finished with you yet, Madam.

[MRS. MANNINGHAM *looks at* BOTH *again, and goes upstairs.*]

ROUGH. [*Pause. To chair down Right.*] You know, I believe you're wrong there, Manningham. I believe that is just what you have done.

MR. MANNINGHAM. Done what?

ROUGH. Finished with your wife, my friend. [*He sits down easily in armchair.*]

MR. MANNINGHAM. [*Crosses to front of table.*] Now, sir—will you have the goodness to tell me your name and your business if any?

ROUGH. I have no name, Manningham, in my present capacity. I am, as I have pointed out, a mere spirit. Perhaps a spirit of something that you have evaded all your life—but in my case, only a spirit. Will you have a cigar with a spirit? We may have to wait some time.

MR. MANNINGHAM. Are you going to tell me your business, sir, or am I going to fetch a policeman and have you turned out?

ROUGH. [*Rises. Puts cigar back in pocket.*] Ah—an admirable idea. I could have thought of nothing better myself. Yes, fetch a policeman, Manningham, and have me turned out— [*Pause.*] Why do you wait?

MR. MANNINGHAM. Alternatively, sir, I can turn you out myself.

ROUGH. [*Standing and facing him.*] Yes. But why not fetch a policeman?

MR. MANNINGHAM. [*After pause.*] You give me the impression, sir, that you have something up your sleeve. Will you go on with what you were saying?

ROUGH. Yes, certainly. Where was I? Yes. [*Pause.*] Excuse me, Manningham, but do you get the same impression as myself?

[*LIGHT starts down.*]

MR. MANNINGHAM. What impression?

ROUGH [*Goes upstage looking at downstage bracket.*] An impression that the light is going down in this room?

MR. MANNINGHAM. I have not noticed it.

ROUGH. Yes—surely— There—[*Crosses to Left Center then down to Left of table. The LIGHT goes slowly down. As* ROUGH *moves* MANNINGHAM *keeps his eyes on him.*]—Eerie, isn't it? Now we are almost in the dark— Why do you think that has happened? You don't suppose a light has been put on somewhere else— You don't suppose there are other spirits—fellow spirits of mine— spirits surrounding this house now—spirits of justice, even, which have caught up with you at last, Mr. Manningham?

MR. MANNINGHAM. [*A step upstage and his hand on the back of chair Right of table.*] Are you off your head, sir?

ROUGH. No, sir. Just an old man seeing ghosts. It must

be the atmosphere of this house. [*Backing away to Left Center as he looks about.*] I can see them everywhere. It's the oddest thing. Do you know one ghost I can see, Mr. Manningham? You could hardly believe it.

MR. MANNINGHAM. What ghost do you see, pray?

ROUGH. Why, it's the ghost of an old woman, sir—an old woman who once lived in this house, who once lived in this very room. Yes—in this very room. What things I imagine!

MR. MANNINGHAM. What are you saying?

ROUGH. Remarkably clear, sir, I see it— An old woman getting ready to go to bed—here in this very room—an old woman getting ready to go up to bed at the end of the day. Why! There she is. She sits just there. [*Points to chair Right of table.* MANNINGHAM *removes his hand from the chair.*] And now it seems I see another ghost as well. [*Pause. He is looking at* MANNINGHAM.] I see the ghost of a young man, Mr. Manningham—a handsome, tall, well-groomed young man. But this young man has murder in his eyes. Why, God bless my soul, he might be you, Mr. Manningham—he might be you! [*Pause.*] The old woman sees him. Don't you see it all? She screams—screams for help—screams before her throat is cut—cut open with a knife. [*Crosses downstage.*] She lies dead on the floor—the floor of this room —of this house. There! [*Pointing to floor in front of table. Pause.*] Now I don't see that ghost any more.

MR. MANNINGHAM. What's the game, eh? What's your game?

ROUGH. [*Confronting* MANNINGHAM.] But I still see the ghost of the man. I see him, all through the night, as he ransacks the house, hour after hour, room after room, ripping everything up, turning everything out, madly seeking the thing he cannot find. Then years pass and where is he?—[*Goes to table Center.*] Why, sir, is he not back in the same house, the house he ransacked, the house he searched—and does he not now stand before the ghost of the woman he killed—in the room in which he killed her? A methodical man, a patient man, but perhaps he has waited too long. For justice has waited too, and here she is, in my person, to exact her due. And justice found, my friend, in one hour what you sought for fifteen years, and still could not find. See here. Look what she found. [*Goes below desk around to drawer.*] A letter which never reached your wife. Then a brooch which you gave your wife but which she did not appreciate. How wicked of her! But then she didn't know its value. How was she to know that it held the Barlow rubies! There! [*Coming below desk to* MANNINGHAM. *Opening it out.*] See. Twelve thousand pounds' worth before your eyes! There you are, sir. You killed one woman for those and tried to drive another out of her mind. And all the time they lay in your own desk, and all they have brought you is a rope around your neck, Mr. Sydney Power!

MR. MANNINGHAM. [*Pause.*] You seem, sir, to have some very remarkable information. Do you imagine you are going to leave this room with such information in your possession? [*Going up to Left Center doors as though to lock them.*]

ROUGH. [*Away to down Left.*] Do you imagine, sir, that you are going to leave this room without suitable escort?

MR. MANNINGHAM. May I ask what you mean by that?

ROUGH. Only that I have men in the house already. Didn't you realize they had signalled their arrival from above, your own way in, Mr. Manningham, when the lights went down?

MR. MANNINGHAM. [*Pause. He looks at* ROUGH.] Here you— What the devil's this? [*He rushes to the door, where two* POLICEMEN *are standing.*] Ah, Gentlemen— Come in. Come in. Make yourselves at home. Here. [*He makes a plunge. They grab him.*] Leave go of me, will you? Here. Leave go of me! Here's a fine way of going on. Here's a fine way!

[*A struggle ensues.* ROUGH, *seeing help is needed, jerks down the bell-cord. With this, they secure* MANNINGHAM. ROUGH *kicks him in the shins. He falls.*]

ROUGH. [*Taking paper from his pocket. Going up to* MANNINGHAM.] Sydney Charles Power, I have a warrant for your arrest for the murder of Alice Barlow. I should warn you that anything you may say now may be taken down in writing and used as evidence at a later date. Will you accompany us to the station in a peaceful manner? You will oblige us all, and serve your own interests best, Power, by coming with us quietly. [MANNINGHAM *renews struggle.*] Very well—take him away—

[*They are about to take him away when* MRS. MANNINGHAM *comes down the stairs. There is a silence.*]

MRS. MANNINGHAM. Inspector Rough—

[*The two* POLICEMEN *turn so that* MANNINGHAM *faces* MRS. MANNINGHAM.]

ROUGH. [*Going to her.*] Yes, my dear, now don't you think you'd better—

MRS. MANNINGHAM. [*In a weak voice.*] Inspector—

ROUGH. Yes?

MRS. MANNINGHAM. I want to speak to my husband.

ROUGH. Now, surely, there's nothing to be—

MRS. MANNINGHAM. I want to speak to my husband.

ROUGH. Very well, my dear, what do you want to say?

MRS. MANNINGHAM. I want to speak to him alone.

ROUGH. Alone?

MRS. MANNINGHAM. Yes, alone. Won't you please let me speak to him alone? I beg of you to allow me. I will not keep him long.

ROUGH. [*Pause.*] I don't quite understand. Alone?— [*Pause.*] Very well. You may speak to him alone. [*He crosses to chair Right of table. To* POLICEMEN.] Very well. Make him fast in this chair. [*He signifies that they are to tie him to chair. They do so and exit Left Center.*] This is anything but in order—but we will wait outside. [MRS. MANNINGHAM *crosses to desk.* ROUGH *examines fastenings on* MANNINGHAM *and crosses up to door, Left Center.*] I'm afraid you must not be long, Mrs. Manningham.

MRS. MANNINGHAM. I do not want you to listen.

ROUGH. No, I will not listen. [ROUGH *hesitates, then exits Left Center.*]

[MRS. MANNINGHAM *looking at her husband. At last she goes over to Left Center door, locks it and then comes to him.*]

MRS. MANNINGHAM. Jack! Jack! What have they done to you? What have they done?

MR. MANNINGHAM. [*Struggling at his bonds, half whispering.*] It's all right, Bella. You're clever, my darling. Terribly clever. Now get something to cut this. I can get out through the dressing-room window and make a jump for it. Can you fetch something?

MRS. MANNINGHAM. [*Hesitating. Crossing to him.*] Yes—yes. I can get something. What can I get?

MR. MANNINGHAM. I've just remembered— There's a razor in my dressing-room. Quick! Can you get it, Bella?

MRS. MANNINGHAM. [*Feverishly.*] Razor—yes—I'll get it for you.

MR. MANNINGHAM. Hurry—yes— In my dresser— Hurry— Quick and get it.

[*She goes into room up Right, talking and mumbling and comes back with the razor and crosses to desk. As she takes the razor from case, a scrap of paper falls to the floor. She stoops to pick it up, almost unconsciously tidy. She glances at it and a happy smile illuminates her face.*]

MRS. MANNINGHAM. [*Joyously.*] Jack! Here's the grocery bill! [*She comes to him, the grocery bill in one hand, the razor in the other. She is half weeping, half laughing.*] You see, dear, I didn't lose it. I told you I didn't!

MR. MANNINGHAM. [*Uncomfortably.*] Cut me loose, Bella.

MRS. MANNINGHAM. [*She stares at him for a moment, then at the grocery bill, then back at him.*] Jack—how did this get in here? You said that I— [*Her voice trails off, a wild look comes into her eyes.*]

MR. MANNINGHAM. [*Trying to placate her with charm.*]

I must have been mistaken about the bill. Now— Quickly, dear, use the razor! Quick!

[*She stares at him for a moment, then moves a step closer. His look falls upon the razor. He glances up at her and a momentary hint of terror comes into his face. He draws back in the chair.*]

MRS. MANNINGHAM. Razor? What razor? [*She holds it up, under his face.*] You are not suggesting that this is a razor I hold in my hand? Have you gone mad, my husband?

MR. MANNINGHAM. Bella, what are you up to?

MRS. MANNINGHAM. [*With deadly rage that is close to insanity.*] Or is it I who am mad? [*She throws the razor from her.*] Yes. That's it. It's I. Of course, it was a razor. Dear God—I have lost it, haven't I? I am always losing things. And I can never find them. I don't know where I put them.

MR. MANNINGHAM. [*Desperately.*] Bella.

[*WARN CURTAIN*]

MRS. MANNINGHAM. I must look for it, mustn't I? Yes —if I don't find it you will lock me in my room—you will lock me in the mad-house for my mischief. [*Her voice is compressed with bitterness and hatred.*] Where could it be now? [*Turns and looks around to Right.*] Could it be behind the picture? Yes, it must be there! [*She goes to the picture swiftly and takes it down.*] No, it's not there—how strange! I must put the picture back. I have taken it down, and I must put it back. There. [*She puts it back askew.*] Where now shall I look? [*She is raging like a hunted animal. Turns and sees the desk.*] Where shall I look? The desk. Perhaps I put it in the desk. [*Goes to the desk.*] No—it is not there—how strange! But here is a letter. Here is a watch. And a bill— See I've found them at last. [*Going to him.*] You see! But they don't help you, do they? And I am trying to help you, aren't I?—to help you escape— But how can a mad woman help her husband to escape? What a pity— [*Getting louder and louder.*] If I were not mad I could have helped you—if I were not mad, whatever you had done, I could have pitied and protected you! But because I am mad I have hated you, and because I am mad I am rejoicing in my heart—without a shred of pity —without a shred of regret—watching you go with glory in my heart!

MR. MANNINGHAM. [*Desperately.*] Bella!

MRS. MANNINGHAM. Inspector! Inspector! [*Up to door —pounds on door then flings it open.*] Come and take this man away! Come and take this man away! [ROUGH *and the others come in swiftly.* MRS. MANNINGHAM *is completely hysterical and goes down to lower end of desk.*] Come and take this man away!

[ROUGH *gestures to the men. They remove* MANNING-HAM. MRS. MANNINGHAM *stands apart, trembling with homicidal rage.* ROUGH *takes her by the shoulders sternly. She struggles to get away. He slaps her across the face. She is momentarily stunned.* ELIZABETH *enters, quickly takes the situation. Gets a glass of water from table up Right and brings it down to* MRS. MANNINGHAM *and gives her a drink.* ROUGH *stands at Left Center watching them for a second and—*]

ROUGH. [*His eyes on* MRS. MANNINGHAM *whose wild fury has resolved in weeping. He leads her to chair Left of table where she sits.*] Now, my dear, come and sit down. You've had a bad time. I came in from nowhere and gave you the most horrible evening of your life. Didn't I? The most horrible evening of anybody's life, I should imagine.

MRS. MANNINGHAM. The most horrible? Oh, no,—the most wonderful.—Far and away the most wonderful.

CURTAIN

FURNITURE—DRAPERIES—PROPERTIES

1 brown carpet to cover entire stage
1 rug in front of fireplace—*closely tacked down*
Stairs covered with carpet
Old-fashioned lace curtains on windows in the bay—the
    downstage lace curtain tacked back near the top to
    let in the light of spot
Velvet drapes on the windows and bay arch—dull red
Lambrakin on mantel-shelf—same material as drapes
Coal grate in fireplace
Lump soft coal in grate
Ashes on hearth under grate
Set of fire tools upper end of fireplace
Coal hod lower end fireplace
Coal in coal hod
Fire tongs in hod
One piece of coal fix in tongs
Large mirror on wall over fireplace
Large ornament on C. of mantel shelf
Pair of vases—one each end of mantel—the one on the
    upper end containing the Barlow rubies
Small mirror lower end of mantel—face down—for use
    of Mrs. Manningham
Small comb—lower end of mantel—for use of Mrs.
    Manningham
Match box—upper end of mantel
Matches in match box
2 small bronze ornaments—one each end of mantel
1 single chair—below fireplace

Secretary against wall above fireplace— Secretary has 2 or more drawers below; 2 doors above and shelves inside

Loose papers in upstage drawer of secretary

Loose papers in downstage drawer of secretary

Medicine box in downstage drawer of secretary

Medicine powders in medicine box

3 drinking glasses on 2nd shelf of secretary

Smelling salts bottle on 2nd shelf of secretary

Books and papers on lower and upper shelf of secretary

Letter file on top of secretary—lower end—standing up—used to hide spotlight

1 velvet family album on downstage end of outside shelf of secretary

Some writing paper on upstage end of outside shelf of secretary

1 bust on top of secretary

1 painting over U. R. door

1 picture on backing of U. R. door

1 single chair under picture on backing U. R.

1 pedestal and statue in corner L. of U. R. door

1 small wall table against stairs above couch

1 painting on wall between stairs and U. L. C. doors

1 pair of pictures below single picture on wall between stairs and U. L. C. doors— The picture to the left of this pair is hung on a nail with cord as it must be easily put up and taken down

1 key in L. door of U. L. C. doors

1 wall table against backing U. L. C. hall

1 pair candle sticks on wall table U. L. C. hall

1 center piece on wall table U. L. C. hall

1 tapestry on wall above the wall table U. L. C. hall

2 crossed swords on tapestry above wall table U. L. C. hall

1 square picture on wall L. of double doors
1 oval old-fashioned framed flowers—below square picture on wall L. of double doors
1 pedestal in corner above bay window
1 vase of withered leaves on pedestal above bay window
1 framed picture on pedestal above bay window
1 table desk with 2 drawers in front of bay window—
    1 drawer upstage—1 drawer downstage
1 student's lamp on upper end of table desk
1 ink stand on table desk
1 pen holder on table desk
1 small Bible—on desk above ink stand
1 trick breakaway under drawer in desk—Act II
1 single chair above table desk
1 armchair back of table desk
1 single chair below table desk against the wall
1 oblong oval table at stage Center
1 lamp on upper end of C-table fastened to table
1 table cover on C-table
2 single chairs on each side of Center table—the chair on the R. of the C-table must be reinforced
1 antimacassar on back of each chair
1 couch at D. R.
1 fancy pillow-cushion on couch
1 London newspaper on couch—Act I and II
1 foot stool in front of couch—Act I and II
1 velvet bell pull fastened to wall near ceiling L. of U. R. C. doors—firmly fastened Act I and II—breakaway Act III

Off stage—R. of U. L. C. doors
    1 long narrow property table
    1 composition black oval tea tray 15" x 20" on prop table—Act I

1 tray doilie . . . . on tray
1 tea pot . . . . " "
1 cream pitcher . . . . " "
1 sugar bowl . . . . " "
1 hot water pitcher . . . . " "
2 small plates . . . . " "
2 cups and saucers . . . . " "
3 spoons . . . . " "
2 small knives . . . . " "
1 small salt receptacle . . . . . . " "
salt in salt receptacle . . . . . . " "
sugar—small cube lumps—in bowl . . . " "
milk—in pitcher . . . . " "
water in pitcher—5 glasses full . . . . " "
2 tea napkins . . . . " "
1 covered muffin dish on property table—Act I
2 muffins in dish—Act I
1 small tray on property table—Act III
1 pitcher of milk on tray—Act III
1 glass on tray—Act III
1 small plate on tray—Act III
Crackers on plate tray—Act III
1 street vendor's bell off stage L.—Act I
1 chime—"Big Ben" off stage L. Act I—III
1 " hammer
9 rubies in vase on upstage end of mantel—Act II
1 lady's watch and chain in upstage drawer of desk—
  Act II
1 brooch in upstage drawer of desk—this brooch opens
  and must have depth to hold rubies—Act II
1 letter in upstage desk drawer—this letter in a mailed
  envelope and has been opened—Act II
1 razor in case off stage U. R.—Act III
1 glass of water on small table against stair—Act III

1 small paper—grocery bill in razor case—Act III

1 door slam off stage U. L.

1 clock strike off stage D. R.

1 sewing box on chair L. of C. table—Act I

sewing materials in sewing box—Act I

1 small change purse in sewing box—Act I

several small coins in purse—Act I

1 brass jardiniere of green plant—Act I—in bay window

HAND PROPS

For Mr. Manningham:

1 watch chain

1 key ring for R. end of watch chain

2 desk keys on chain

For Rough:

1 warrant for arrest

1 pocket key ring with keys and gadgets on it

1 white ½ pint flask with cork stopper

Liquor for flask

3 different sized "jimmies"

1 dark-colored material used as wrapper for the "jimmies"

1 jeweler's eye glass

2 cigars

1 watch and chain

LIGHTING INFORMATION

Illumination of the scene is supposedly by gas and from three sources. Stage Left area is from a student lamp on the desk; stage Center is from a lamp on the Center table; and stage Right from two wall brackets. The two wall brackets each have two circuits in them, one on a light amber circuit of two bulbs and the other circuit is three bulbs in white. The bulbs are the smallest obtainable such as are used on Christmas trees. Each circuit in each bracket is on separate control and, in addition, the two white circuits are on a master control. At the original lighting of the brackets in Act I by Nancy the light amber flashes up, then out, then the white circuit comes up and from then on the white circuit goes up and down on the dimmer as the lines and business in the script indicate. The table lamp and desk lamp are each a single, light straw bulb, larger than the brackets and on a dimmer and each separately controlled. It is the lighting and dimming of these units that control the spot lighting of their respective areas.

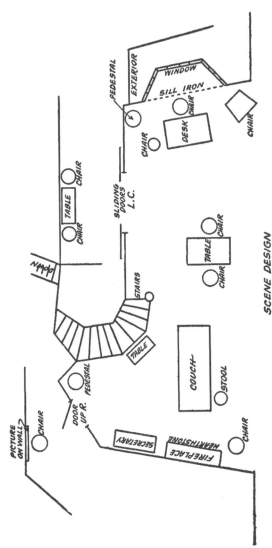

SCENE DESIGN
"ANGEL STREET"